MIDLIFE WOLF BITE

ACCIDENTAL ALPHA · BOOK 1

CARISSA ANDREWS

DEDICATION

I know I dedicate books a lot to my PA Jenny Bodle, but really, this book would not exist without her encouragement.

I was never a werewolf kinda girl. However, Ella and Stone are changing my mind. Werewolves are kinda hot.

Thanks for the push, Jenny!

CHAPTER 1
DIVORCE BITES

ELLA

Anyone who tells you divorce can be amicable is straight-up lying to your face.

Divorce with kids involved? Yeah, you may as well leave the planet because every move you make is going to be open for scrutiny.

Whether you're a good person or not, doesn't mean a damn thing because in someone's worldview, you're the villain, and that's all that matters.

Practically driving on autopilot, I stare across the green, hilly landscape. Over and over I've prayed this move will be the right decision.

For all of us.

In my youth, I'd done some pretty spontaneous, albeit kinda crazy things... I took a drive to downtown Chicago by myself, with no cellphone—no protection of any kind, actually—all because I wanted to see the sights for myself. I slept with a guy once without even knowing his name. And my favorite stupid, spontaneous decision: I got married before I turned twenty.

But this?

Well, let's just say it's the craziest thing I've done in a good long while. Maybe ever.

When my best friend and resident vicarious-liver, Denise, suggested I buy a house off the internet an entire state away, I thought she was nuts. Hell, she probably *is* nuts.

But I did it anyway.

So, what's that say about me? I mean, sure, getting as far away as possible from the ex drove the bus on that decision. I'm not even gonna lie.

But regardless, I still knew it was bonkers. I've never even seen the house in person. We could turn up to a total dump and be stuck with it. At this point, it would be my luck.

On the other hand, if the house is as cool as it seemed from the pics, then this could be the adventure of a lifetime. At least my kids didn't think I was too insane. So, that's saying something. Or maybe they just wanted to get some distance, too.

"How much further is this place?" Asher asks, repositioning in the passenger seat. He tugs his hood down over his eyebrows, then tips his head to the glass on his passenger side door.

My eyes flick to the in-dash GPS and I arch my aching back.

Lord, I'm too old for such a long drive.

"It says we're nearly there. Another twenty minutes," I mutter, rolling my head from one side to the other.

Both daughter and son groan in unison.

"*Another* twenty minutes?" Avery says, leaning in between the console from the backseat. "Is that in *actual* time? Because I swear you said twenty minutes forty minutes ago."

I spit out a laugh. "Is the TikToker going through filming withdrawals?"

"*Mom*," she says, vanishing back into her seat.

I can practically hear her roll her eyes.

"Are you kidding? She's been filming this whole trip," Asher says, snickering under his breath. "Can't you hear her making duck faces?"

Lightning fast, Avery's right hand snakes out and slaps her brother across the upper arm. "*Shut up.*"

"Hey," Asher says, twisting around to take a crack at hitting her back.

I thrust my arm out as a divider between the two of them.

"Guys, *enough*," I say, busting out the 'mom voice' so they knew I mean business. "I know you're both ready to get out of this cramped vehicle. I am, too. But we need to hold our shit together or Mom's gonna lose *her* shit and *trust me*, that won't be pretty. My ass is already numb and I'm pretty sure I won't be able to walk straight for a week. Now's not the time to get on my bad side."

"Yeah, you heard Mom. Knock it off," Avery says. In the rearview mirror I witness her tongue flash out like she's four and not fourteen. Without a word, I lower my eyebrows when her deep brown eyes find mine.

"Real mature," Asher snorts, swiping his sandy brown hair out of his eyes and turning back to face his window.

My phone vibrates from my cupholder and on instinct, I eye the notification. Of course, it's a text from the evil-one-who-shall-not-be-named. I sigh, fighting the urge to roll my eyes and stick out my own tongue.

Without checking the message, I stare out the windshield and try desperately to focus on the road instead of the knot of dread forming in my stomach.

Honestly, a text from him could only mean one of two things. He wants me to be his personal assistant, likely in an attempt to force our two teenage kids to call him, or he wants to question my parenting skills. Again.

Either way, it's about flexing his *'I'm still the dad'* muscles. Apparently, because he doesn't give a fuck what the court documents say... Or the kids for that matter. Or maybe because he isn't comfortable being irrelevant.

"It's from Dad," Avery mutters, her voice practically a whisper.

"Yeah, I know." I shift my gaze back to the rearview mirror just as she pulls her hood down and tightens

4

the drawstring. She slinks into herself, wrapping her arms tightly around her torso.

God, how did I not realize how bad it was for them?

"What do you think he wants this time?" Asher asks. He might be seventeen, but I can still sense his fear and anxiety as it rolled off him in waves.

"I don't know. Do you want to look for me?" I ask, shooting him a quick glance.

"Not overly," he says, his gaze locked out on the passing trees.

Me either, kid.

I take a deep breath, then flick the phone open to reveal the message.

Are you going to have Asher call me or not?

Ah, so PA it is.

I shake my head, not bothering to respond. Even if I did, he'd find some way to twist it and make it my fault they didn't want to speak to him. God forbid he take any personal responsibility.

Denise was right. I did need a new life. One that turned this mundane existence and flipped it on its head.

Or flipped *him* on *his.*

I'm not picky.

"Why can't he just let us be? Doesn't he realize he's just pissing us off more by being such a dick?" Avery says, her lips twisting to the side of her face.

I shrug. "I honestly don't know. If I could make sense out of that man's brain, pretty sure we wouldn't be where we are now."

"It's because he doesn't actually give a fuck about anyone else," Asher says, venom leaking into his voice.

"Language," I hiss, twisting to give him a fixed stare.

"Sorry," he says, without even looking back at me. "But it's true."

I reach out, placing a hand on his shoulder. "I know it seems that way, but—"

My gaze returns to the road just in time to see an enormous white wolf race out in front of our vehicle. For the briefest of moments, I marvel at the way its fur contrasts so boldly against the lush green of the landscape.

In the same moment, I grasp the wheel with both hands and slam on the brakes. The tires of our Highlander squeal, launching the stench of burnt rubber into the air.

Asher's head snaps forward and his left hand braced against the dash. "Holy shit. What was that thing?"

My heart pounds in my ears and adrenaline courses

down my arms and legs, making them shake. The wolf, on the other hand, stands just off to the side of the road with its head held high. A shiver races down my spine as its bright green eyes lock with mine. It's almost as if it's inspecting us, rather than the other way around.

"What is that thing? A timber wolf?" Avery chimes in. "It's *massive*."

Swallowing hard, I shake my head and glance at her. "I'm not sure. Maybe?"

By the time I look back, the wolf is gone.

"What's going on up there?" Asher asks, raising his arm to point through the windshield.

With my foot still firmly planted on the brake, I redirect my gaze further out. A black truck up ahead surges forward like he was being chased by hell-hounds or something. Then, with a sharp swerve, it veers into the oncoming lane. Out in front of them is a smaller SUV. Its bright red paint is hard to miss as it swerves slightly to avoid the black truck's erratic movements.

"The road rage is real with that one," Avery says, leaning forward. She presses her hands against both front seats as her eyes lock on the scene.

I nod. "You're not kidding. What the hell are they doing?"

The black truck twists sharply to the right and clips the red SUV's back bumper. The event puts the SUV into a spin. It does a full three-sixty before the driver floors it. The truck, on the other hand, keeps up, staying right on the red SUV's tail.

"Oh my god, they're trying to run that red SUV off the road," I cry, covering my mouth with my fingertips.

"What do we do?" Avery cries.

Snapped back to reality, I reach for my phone and pull up the dial pad. Someone is going to get hurt if this keeps up. We've got to report it.

"Mom, are we safe? What if they come back this way?" Avery asks, panic rising at the edge of her tone.

"Don't worry, honey. I'm sure we're okay," I say, pressing the send button to 911.

Just then, the black truck swerves again, slamming its passenger side into the red SUV. The force is enough to launch the SUV up and over the guardrail on the right-hand side.

My mouth drops open in horror as the SUV rotates forty-five degrees in mid-air, then drops into the ravine and out of view.

CHAPTER 2
THE ONLY WAY
ELLA

"9-1-1, what's your emergency?" The voice on the other end of the phone echoes in my ear.

Unfortunately, I can't seem to get my brain to process what to do next. Instead, I stare in horror and shock at the place where the red SUV plummeted from view.

"Oh my god. Mom, did you see that?" Avery asks, her voice now reaching octaves far higher than normal. "They just flew off the road."

The black truck guns it, racing off as it heads north —and away from us.

Without thinking, I drop my phone down onto the middle console as the tiny metallic voice continues to ring out. I shift into gear and floor it.

"Mom," Asher cries out, grabbing hold of the door handle and squeezing hard. "What are you doing?"

"We need to see if they're okay. I won't let whoever

was in that car die down there alone," I say, my voice cracking, despite my resolve.

My heart thunders in my chest and all I can think about is... What if they have a family? What if it's a whole family in there? Oh my god, what if there are *kids* in that vehicle?

Tears stream down my face by the time I slam on the brakes and shift into park.

"Mom don't go—" Avery says, groping for my seat.

"Honey, I need to check on them," I say, unbuckling my seatbelt and opening my car door.

"Don't leave us here alone," she squeals, pulling on my sleeve. "What if that psycho comes back?"

"Mom, don't go," Asher says, echoing his sister's concerns. He swallows hard, his tough exterior melting away as his whole body shakes.

I glance down and pick up the phone. Shoving it into Asher's hands, I say, "Talk to the dispatcher. Tell them what happened and stay on the line with them until someone from the police arrives. If you see anyone who's not a cop or an ambulance coming down the road, get out of the car and run into the tree-line over there." I point the direction we came from.

"What about the *wolf*?" Avery squeaks, her brown eyes wide with terror.

"Honey, what if there are *kids* down there?" I ask, matching her desperation. "I have to check on them, sweetie. If roles were reversed, I'd want someone to check on us, too. Stay in the car as long as you feel safe.

I'll be right back. *I promise.*" I reach out, pressing my hand to Avery's cheek, then I turn to Asher. I squeeze his shoulder and point to the phone. "Talk to them."

Then, without another word, I close my door and race to the spot where the SUV vanished. Behind me, I hear our Highlander's doors lock—something I taught them to do from a very young age. With a final glance over my shoulder, I mouth, *"love you both,"* then begin my descent down the sharp, rocky landscape.

The sun is low, but the heat from the day is still evident as the humidity pools between my shoulders and trickles down my back after only a minute outside the air-conditioned vehicle.

Huge boulders and rocks make up the area at first and as I make my way down into the ravine, I can't even see the red SUV. However, the further I descend, trees and shrubbery develop and evidence of the wreck becomes apparent. Branches and leaves are scattered all over and the further I go, bigger branches and chunks of plastic, glass, and metal litter the ground.

I see the smoke from the engine before I see the SUV itself. When it comes into view, its front bumper and hood are crumpled so far inward, I can barely make out where the engine was. The vehicle rests at an odd angle, partially on its passenger side, partially tipped downward. Every side of it is crumpled in some way, clearly having rolled its way to this final resting place.

"Hello?" I call out, my voice wavering. "Is anyone there?"

Half of me wants desperately to find them alive, but the other half of me is scared shitless that I'll find them dead. Biting back the rising bile, I edge closer, trying to get a view of the cabin.

The stench of burnt rubber, gasoline, and electricity tickles my nose and I'm suddenly acutely aware of the dangers as I approach.

Could the vehicle explode?

Goodness knows if this were the movies, it would blow the second I get close enough.

A muffled groan escapes from the vehicle and without another thought, I race forward, needing to do whatever it takes to help the person—*or people*—inside.

"Hello?" I repeat as I get to the driver's side door.

Not a single window is left on the vehicle. Instead, the shards are scattered all over the ground, inside the dash, and across the seats. I breathe a sigh of relief when I realize there are no additional passengers inside, but the driver is in desperate need of medical attention.

Blood gushes from his head and he blinks hard to focus on me as I grab hold of the door.

"Oh my god," I breathe, floating my gaze inside the cab.

Not only is he barely coherent, but he's hanging by a thread. The front dashboard is practically resting in his lap and something metallic has been shoved from the engine and lodged itself into the middle of his torso. I swallow hard, forcing down the contents in my stomach that are threatening to come back up.

"*Please,* you have to—" the man begins, extending a bloody left arm out the broken window toward me. His voice is a raspy whisper as he waves to me, urging me to bend closer.

My eyebrows tip up and my heart breaks for him. There's nothing I can do to help save this man. He's going to die and I'm going to be here to witness it.

I clear my throat, trying to be strong for him as I bend in. "I'm so sorry," I whisper.

His chocolate brown eyes are wild with fear and he gropes for my hands. "You have to tell her..." He takes a labored breath, coughing up blood. It spurts across the steering wheel as he turns away from me. When he turns back, the color has drained from his face. "Tell Clem I love her."

I nod, my head bobbing on my neck like a bobble-head. "Of course." I reach out, placing my hand over his extended arm. I have no idea who this Clem is, but I'll do whatever I can to make sure she gets the message.

The man seems appeased by this and his eyes drift closed as he takes a slow, rattly breath from his nose. When his eyes reopen, I double-take, and stumble back. Gone is the chocolate color and instead, his irises have an unearthly golden glow. The hairs on the back of my neck and arms rise and my breath hitches. Every inch of me is screaming to run—*run far away.*

With more energy than I thought he'd be capable of, the man lunges forward in his seat. The sound of metal slicing through meat and bone makes my skin crawl as he reaches out of the vehicle and grabs hold of me. In a swift motion, he pulls me forward until my knees hit the side of the door.

His grip is insanely strong as he holds onto me and even if I wanted to run, I wouldn't be able to. Between his ridiculously strong grasp and the power rolling off of him, my body locks up—clearly going into freeze mode.

God, why can't fight be my go-to-F response?

"I'm sorry," he mutters, blood spewing from his lips. It splatters against my cheek and I tip my face away out of reflex. His golden eyes flash again as he takes another labored breath. "Please believe me—this is the only way."

I clutch at his hand and shake my head. "What is?" I ask, my voice rising with the question.

A heady energy surges, surrounding myself and the man like we're in the middle of a tornado, despite nothing of the sort going on. Before I can do anything, he yanks me closer until I'm practically in the vehicle along with him. Then, in a movement so swift, I barely registered it—his teeth plunge into my bicep.

CHAPTER 3
DOA
ELLA

A scream erupts from my lips as I try to claw myself out of the man's grasp. Blood gushes down my arm, soaking the side of the man's face as it trails to my wrist.

"Let go," I cry, pressing my right hand against the side of his face.

Energy explodes around us, surging like a storm. It shakes the branches and even the birds in the trees scatter. Then, as suddenly as this nightmare began, the man's teeth disengage and he slumps backward in his seat, spent.

I grope at my wound, feeling the rush of blood spurt between my fingertips. Stumbling back, I stare, dumbfounded at the ashen face of the man.

"What the fuck?" I spit, blinking back my horror and surprise.

Stones and pebbles skitter into the ravine and my attention snaps to the right. With all that's happened, my heart is about to leap from my chest and make a run for it. When nothing happens, I shake it off and turn back to the vehicle. The man inside hasn't moved and now I'm scared to death to even check in on him.

Could he be...?

Swallowing hard, I take a tentative step toward him, keeping a close eye on his chest and noting the lack of movement.

Suddenly, the brush to the right moves and another man steps into view. Again, my heart leaps into my throat and within microseconds, I assess whether or not he's a danger. However, the distraught expression he holds tells me he's no threat.

"Are you hurt?" the man asks, rushing over to the scene.

His emerald eyes lock with mine for the briefest of moments as he points to my arm. Something in his discerning gaze makes me feel incredibly uncomfortable. It's like he can see right through to the core of me, stripping me down.

Stray beams of sunlight bounce off his dark brown hair, creating a soft glow of red and gold in the depths. Streaks of gray tickle at his temples, hinting at his age being closer to my own.

It's then that I realize he must have been swimming nearby or something. He's clad in a pair of Hawaiian swim trunks—*and that's it.*

Despite myself, I stare in awe at the sheer masculinity of his upper body. He sports a golden tan and more muscle on a man than I've seen in my entire life—unless of course, you count all the covers of smutty books I keep on my ebook reader. Goodness knows the ex didn't come with pecs like that.

Snaking up his arms are dark tattoos, but from this distance it's hard to tell what any of them mean without totally staring.

And boy, I wouldn't mind staring...

He also has a bold, tribal moon tattoo seared into his chest on the left hand side.

"Miss?" he says, taking another step closer and snapping his fingers in front of my face. "Are you all right?"

I shake my head, coming to my senses. "No—I mean, yes. I'm fine. It's him you should be worried about. Someone ran him off the road. I think he might be..." My voice squeaks with emotion. Why can't I ever hold myself together?

The man looks over his shoulder, his eyes scanning the man in the SUV. Without even checking for a pulse, he declares, "He's gone."

My mouth gapes open. "But how can you be so sure? I mean—"

"I can just tell. It's in the air," he says, taking a deep breath and turning back to me. There's a hint of sorrow buried in his expression.

"Did you," I begin, glancing at the body of the man in the SUV, "know him?"

He takes a beat, his head dropping slightly before whispering, "Yeah. I knew him."

"Oh, shit. I'm so sorry. I came down as soon as I saw what happened. We called 9-1-1." I point up toward the street.

The man glances the direction of my finger, his lashes beating against his cheeks with his thoughts. Suddenly, he glances back at me, his jaw hardening. "What happened there?" He tips his chin toward my arm.

"I got a little too close," I say, still holding onto my bicep. "He must have been delirious because he bit me. I just hope I don't turn into a zombie or something now." I laugh awkwardly, trying to make light of a situation that's turned far too grim for my comfort.

God, I suck at intense situations.

The man's dark eyebrows knit together, but he doesn't say anything.

I clear my throat. "Joke. It was a joke."

"Ah," he says. Tilting his head like he has some sort of supersonic hearing, he closes his eyes. "You should go."

"The paramedics should be on their way. I want to make sure he's—"

"I got this," the man says, his face hardening until it's devoid of any kind of emotion.

"But, the police—" I rebut.

"I saw what happened here, too. I can take care of it," he says more forcefully as he reaches out, spinning me toward the way I came.

"Hang on a second," I spit, spinning myself back around. "I didn't see you. If you saw the whole thing, where were you?"

"In the woods," he says, as if it's completely obvious.

"Looking like that?" I say, before I can help myself.

The guy actually smirks at me. "Is there a dress code for nature?"

I take a step back, flustered. "Well, no. It's just that—"

"Look, you're shaken up. I get it. This was pretty traumatic. I'm just trying to help out so you don't have to worry about all of this," he says, trying too hard to sound reasonable.

However, after years of dealing with the ex, I know a condescending tone when I hear one.

I plaster on a smile. "Well, thank you for your concern, but I think I'll just stay here until the authorities arrive. Besides, I need to deliver a message for him." I point to the dead guy and try not to shudder.

Tall, tanned, and egotistical steps into my space. "What message?"

I hold my ground, pressing my fingertips against his rock-hard pecs in the hopes it will make him take a step back. He doesn't budge.

"The message isn't for you," I spit, refusing to be the first to move.

He makes a noise that sounds suspiciously like a growl.

I jut my chin out and place my hands on my hips. I can be a stubborn ass when I want to be, and for whatever reason, this guy is pressing down all those buttons.

Thankfully, he takes a blissful step back, giving me a chance to breathe. Then, he turns, pinching the bridge of his nose. "How do you know the message wasn't for me?"

"Well, for starters, you don't look much like a *her*," I say, casting him a knowing look.

Relief floods his features. "It was for Clem?"

I pinch my lips tight.

He nods to himself, apparently happy with my reaction.

Jerk.

"Well, how are you going to get the message to her if you don't even know who she is?" the guy asks.

"I'm resourceful," I say, shrugging.

"Sure," he nods. "Or...you could give me the message and I can pass it on to her."

"How do I know I could even trust you?" I fire back.

His eyes flash a warning. "You don't."

A shudder involuntarily skitters up my spine, but my vision swims slightly. I fight back the urge to sit down.

"Are you okay?" the man asks, reaching out for me.

"I'm fine," I say, batting back his hands.

"It doesn't look that way to me."

My eyebrows rise of their own accord and I shoot him a pointed stare. "Yeah, well, looks can be deceiving."

His features tighten again and he takes another step back.

Must have hit a nerve. *Good.*

"If you're Mr. Know-It-All, who's Clem and how do I find her?" I say, trying hard not to let by body sway.

"She's my sister," he says matter-of-factly.

My gaze floats back to the dead guy. "He was your brother-in-law?"

The man's nostrils flare and his face screws up a bit before leveling out. "Yeah," he says, refusing to meet my stare.

"Shit. Now I feel like an ass," I mutter, turning around.

Leave it to me to go all defiant on a grieving man. No wonder he's such a jerk right now.

A piercing howl cuts through the relative silence of the woods and the pitch makes every nerve in my body turn into a live wire.

I spin around. "We saw a huge timber wolf before all of this went down. You don't think—"

"You should go. *Now,*" he says, his green eyes blazing into mine. "I can't protect you here."

"Protect me? What about you?" I say. It's not like

he has a gun or something buried in those swim trunks.

"Go—" the man barks out. "I've got this."

He no sooner says the words when a pack of three of the largest wolves I've ever seen burst into the ravine, their hackles raised and teeth bared.

CHAPTER 4

RUN FOR YOUR LIFE
ELLA

E very cell in my body screams to *run*. Run far, run fast, and never look back.

But my damn feet refuse to move. Goddamn freeze response.

"Go," the man growls at me, turning his back to me as he focuses on the three wolves as they spread out and begin to circle.

One of the wolves snarls, snapping his teeth as it lunges forward. The man widens his stance, his broad shoulders popping in anticipation.

"Are you deaf? Get out of here." The desperation in the man's voice knocks something loose inside my brain.

Who am I? I'm no fucking hero. If anything, I'd be in his way.

A single thought cycles through my mind: *Get help*.

Without another thought, I turn from the mangled

car, the dead man, and the one ready to take on three damn scary wolves. I take off running, racing from the ravine and back the way I'd come.

With any luck, the police and paramedics will be here and they'll be able to do something about the wolves. If nothing else, the police should have guns...

Loud snarls and the snapping of multiple jaws erupt behind me and it pushes me to run faster. My quads scream as I climb back up the rocky landscape. The whole time I pray the wolves don't follow me. I'm too old to give up much of a fight. But I also pray that the man in the swim trunks will be okay. He's barely got a stitch of clothing on to protect him from the ferocity of those wolves.

Numerous times, I trip over my own two feet as I clamber over the loose gravel and boulders on my way up to the road. By the time I reach the top, my body is quaking from the burst of adrenaline and sheer terror.

"Mom—" Avery screams as she kicks open the door to the backseat of our Highlander.

The beautiful sound of sirens greets me as I collapse into my daughter's arms. Before I know it, Asher is there, too, his gangly teenager arms wrapping around us both.

"What happened down there?" Asher asks, his voice barely a whisper as he squeezes tighter. "Are you hurt?"

"I'm fine. But the driver—" I say, fighting back the

fresh tears springing to my eyes as grief and relief mix together. "The driver's dead and the wolves—"

Avery pulls back. "There were wolves down there?"

I nod. "There's another man. He saw the whole thing, too, but he's still down there. He's trying to..." Swallowing hard, I push up to a stand and wave my arms for the ambulance. "We need to get him some help."

"There's another guy?" Asher repeats.

The ambulance comes to a halt right behind our vehicle just as two squad cars pull in.

I nod to Asher but make my way to the emergency personnel.

A female cop is the first to step out, her red hair pulled back into a tight bun at the back of her head.

"Please," I say, pointing to the ravine, "there's a man down there and three wolves—"

"Did you say wolves?" A male cop says, hopping out of the driver's side. His build is slight compared to the man down in the ravine and all I can think about is... Does he have it in him to take down these animals?

I nod. "Yes, he's protecting the body of the driver. Please, someone needs to help him—"

"Don't worry ma'am. We got this from here," the male cop says, holding out his hand and tipping his chin. His blond hair catches the sunlight, turning it golden.

Without another word, the two police officers descend into the ravine. Both have guns strapped to their hips and I can only hope they'll be enough to scare off the wolves or put them down, if it comes to that. Two more police officers hop out of the other vehicle and descend the hillside without even so much as glancing at me or my kids.

From the back of the ambulance, two male paramedics hop out, carrying some sort of lightweight gurney. One of them reaches inside the vehicle and grabs a briefcase-looking thing. I can only assume it's some sort of medkit. They also follow after the police officers.

From the front seat of the ambulance, a female driver with dark brown skin and black hair hops out. The woman makes her way to us, while a guy with shaggy brown hair hops out of the passenger side and walks around to the back of the ambulance.

"Are you hurt?" the woman asks as she reaches us. Her dark brown eyes are disarming, and her open expression instantly makes me feel safe. She lifts her hand, pointing to my bloody arm.

"Yeah, it's not a big deal, though," I say, still groping at my bicep. The aching from the bite has diminished a little bit, but I know these sorts of things can be deceiving. Humans have some of the dirtiest mouths on the planet—and we're not just talking about their language, either.

"Well, let's take a quick look at it before the others come back," she offers, tipping her head toward the back of the ambulance.

Nodding, the kids and I follow behind her. The other paramedic is busy getting various things pulled out and in place, clearly thinking there will be something other than a body to treat. I can only hope that's true for the man left down there. My stomach rolls and I turn to face the woman again. I take a seat on the floor of the ambulance, my feet dangling over the edge of the vehicle.

"Let me take a look at that," she offers, reaching out for my arm.

Avery and Asher stand back, their dark eyes wide and fearful as they watch us. Nodding to the woman, I extend my arm as she pulls out some cotton balls and a bottle of some sort of cleaning solution. The odor is terrible as she cracks open the bottle.

"Wanna tell me what happened?" The woman asks, wiping gingerly at the wound, which sizzles as it comes into contact with the liquid.

"A man got run off the road. His vehicle is down at the bottom of the ravine there..." I begin.

"No, I mean with your arm," the paramedic says, her voice soft and even as her eyes stay glued to her work.

"Oh, right." I shake my head. "Well, the man wasn't in his right mind. He was pinned by some metallic something or other. He bit me," I say, remembering back to the horror of the moment.

Her eyebrows tug in and she looks up. "He bit you?"

Again, I nod. "Yeah. Right before he died."

The dark-haired guy stops his work and the two paramedics exchange a significant glance.

"But I'm really worried about the other guy down there. He saw everything from the woods and came running. But three wolves came out of nowhere—"

"I wouldn't worry. We're trained in this area on how to deal with the wolves," the male paramedic says, kneeling down beside me.

"Well, it doesn't look like this wound is too bad. Should heal up just fine in a couple of days," the woman paramedic says.

"Are you sure?" I say, eyeing my bicep. Coulda fooled me with the amount of blood that flowed from the bite. I thought for sure I'd need a tetanus shot or something.

Weird.

"Yeah, look," she says, wiping away the crimson remnants. Bite marks are there, sure, but they barely look like they punctured the skin. "You were lucky."

Maybe all the blood was from the dead guy's mouth. I mean, he had to be bleeding internally with that metal spike through his body. Right?

"Huh," I mutter.

The paramedic places a bandage across my bicep and pats my knee. "You should be good to go."

I sit up straighter, my gaze drifting out over the broken guardrail. "Should we stay here until..."

She shakes her head. "No need. We have the emergency call on file. If the police need more, they'll be in touch. I'm sure they'll have enough to deal with right now."

I inhale sharply. I'm sure dealing with dead bodies and families definitely comes first, but I could have sworn from all the cop shows I've watched, they'd want the eye-witnesses to stay until they've taken their statement. But that's television and this is real life.

"Yeah, okay," I say, hopping down from the ambulance.

She shoots me a reassuring smile as she steps back.

Both Asher and Avery rush forward, invading my personal space like they're two and four years old again.

"Can we go now?" Avery asks, wrapping her arm through my non-bandaged one.

"Yeah, let's go. I could use a hot bath and a glass of wine," I mutter, wanting to put this entire thing behind me. But before I can help myself, I twist back around. "What about the man down there?"

The woman's forehead crinkles. "What about him?"

"How can I find out if he's okay?"

A smile graces her face, lighting it up. "Oh, I'm sure when the police follow up with you, they'll be able to fill you in. Right now, what's important is clearing the scene so we can all stay focused."

"Right, right..." I say, her words tumbling around

in my head. Shouldn't they at least be taking a statement from me? Maybe grab my name and address?

As ready as I am to get the hell out of Dodge, my thoughts are pulled to the half-naked man in the ravine. I don't know what it is about him, but I feel responsible for him—like I need to make sure he's okay. But it's not like I have any control over what happens to him from this point forward.

I've done all I can. Help is on its way.

So, why do I still feel so anxious?

CHAPTER 5
TABULA RASA
ELLA

Silence expands between the three of us as we continue on with our journey. My mind pulls me back into the current of recent events and I can't believe this is the *start* to our "fresh start." I hope it's not an ominous sign that we should have stayed in California.

Avery is the first to break the silence. "Do you think we're safe?" she asks, echoing my own concerns as she plucks at her hoodie's strings.

My lips tug down and nostrils flare under my inhalation. "I honestly don't know. I *hope* so. But this doesn't bode well, does it?"

Asher snickers, thrusting his hands under his armpits. "Welcome to our lives, Mom. Glad you could join us."

I inhale deeply, holding the breath in for a moment before exhaling out as much of my anxiety as possible.

"You know what? Screw this. We aren't going to let this bring us down. This is a mind over matter thing," I say, holding up my index finger and going into motivational speaker mode. "It was a total fluke occurrence and we need to treat it as such. I mean, come on... We're on the way to our new house to start our next big adventure, dammit. That's *exciting*."

"Yay, new house," Avery says, mustering up some enthusiasm. Unfortunately, it falls a bit flat.

Asher doesn't even make a move.

My shoulders slump in defeat. "Come on guys. It's going to be great. Wait until you see this house. It's incredible."

"I'm just looking forward to getting in my own bed. When were the movers supposed to be there?" Asher says, glancing my direction. "Please tell me it's today."

"Child, do you ever listen to a word I say? I mean, do I just talk for my own fun or what?" I say, throwing him a look of annoyance.

"They were moving our stuff in yesterday, dufus," Avery says, shaking her head. "That's why we took the scenic route. Remember?"

I jab my thumb toward the backseat. "See? She listens."

"There's a first time for everything," Asher mutters.

"Hey—" Avery starts, reaching between the front seats to slap her brother on the arm.

He twists around to retaliate, but I thrust my arm out before he can do anything. "Enough. Good god, how old are the two of you? Besides, faces forward. We're here."

In the rear view mirror, I catch Avery making a face when Asher turns to look out the front window.

Lord help me, this constant bickering has to come to an end soon. Right?

I flip the blinker on and turn right onto the short driveway. It leads up to the small one stall garage to the right of the adorable turn-of-the-century Craftsman home. Its soft green vinyl siding, clearly an upgrade from recent tenants, is almost an extension of the green grass and wooded yard. A subtly lighter green, almost yellow, surrounds the wider trim of the windows and base of the building. It also runs up the columns of the open air porch and the underside of the roof's overhang. Without the subtle pop of burnt red trimwork on the front step railings and around the inner portion of the windows, the home could have faded completely into its surroundings.

"This is totally cute," Avery says, pulling herself forward to see between the two front seats.

"I know, right?" I say, pulling up in front of the garage door painted in the same colors and put the vehicle in park.

Asher quirks an eyebrow. "It looks awfully girly."

"Well, a *girl* did pick it out." I smirk.

Asher groans.

"Oh, come on. It's adorable and I plan to grow old and die here, so it needs to fit *me*, not you. Besides, it's way bigger than the apartment we were in."

"*Anything* is bigger than that apartment," he retorts.

"You're not wrong. But wait until you see the inside. You won't care how adorably girly it is from the outside." I reach out and pat his arm. "Trust me."

His expression remains flat, riding the wave of his skepticism.

Avery, on the other hand, is out of the backseat before I even reach for my door handle. I grab my cellphone and follow after her.

"Mom—oh my god, look at this... There's flowers and everything," she squeals with delight, bending down and caressing one of the many yellow irises. She's my nature lover and I knew she'd be excited about the gardens. It makes me excited to see what she thinks of the backyard.

"There are?" I rush over, feigning surprise as I kneel down beside her. "Look, Asher. *Flowers.*" I point at them, grinning like a lunatic.

Despite himself, a grin cracks through his grumpy teenage boy façade.

"See, it'll grow on you," I say, clasping my hands to my chest and blinking sweetly.

"That's not why I'm smiling," he says, lowering his eyebrows in mock seriousness.

I stand up, brushing off my thighs. "Oh, really. Then why the smile, pray tell?"

He holds my gaze for a beat, then mumbles, "It's nice to see you happy for a change." He thrusts his hands into the front pockets of his jeans and drops his gaze to the ground.

My heart squishes and I can't help the tears that spring to my eyes.

"Oh, god. Now you've gone and made her cry. Nice job, dummy," Avery says, rolling her eyes. "You couldn't just keep it about the flowers."

I wipe away my emotions. "I'm not crying. I'm totally fine."

"Uh-huh," Avery grunts.

Asher clears his throat. "So, are you gonna show us the inside of this granny cottage, or what?"

"Granny cottage... Psh. I'll have you know this is a *Craftsman*."

"You say that like it means something, Mom. We don't speak realtor," Avery says, walking up the front steps and peering in through the windows on either side of the front door. "Holy shit—"

"Avery," I say, coming up behind her, "*language*."

"Seriously, mom. This place is incredible. Are you sure we can afford this thing?" she sputters, her nose practically flattened against the glass.

I jangle the key given to me at the closing. "I wouldn't have this if it weren't already a done deal. Step aside, Minion."

I shoo her with my hand, making way for the magical moment of opening the door to our new home for the very first time. For a second, though, I clutch the keys to my chest, savoring the occasion. After the months of upheaval, the desperation and denial leading up to the divorce, and then all the shit we've dealt with lately... I can hardly believe we're actually *here*.

Granted, I have no idea how I got such awesome luck on this house. I like to consider it the fate of the universe guiding me here. Otherwise, it means it was a crack house or it's haunted or something and if that's the case, I don't want to know. Blissful ignorance will be my go-to.

"Is everyone ready?" I whisper, keeping with the reverence of the moment.

"Mom, I have to take a dump," Asher says. "Can we just go in already?"

I sigh, dropping my head to my chest. "And the moment's over. Come on."

Without another word, I slide the key into the lock and twist the handle. I push the door open wide, letting them go in before me since I want to gauge their reactions to the house. I already know it's beautiful, but now I hope they see it, too.

My stomach twists itself into a flurry of activity. It's almost like Christmas Day giddiness. The kids always thought the best part was opening their presents, but I swear the best part was being the parent and seeing their faces when they got something they *really* loved.

Please let this be something they really love.

"Wow," Avery's voice echoes from the main entry way. An air of wonder clings to the word and relief warms my core.

I walk inside, taking in the space as well.

Dark brown, classic damask wallpaper adorns the alcove space like an inviting hug. To the right is the archway leading to the large living room area with a decorative fireplace adorned with a wood surround and red and black tiles. To the left is the large open dining room, with wall to ceiling wood paneling. And directly in front of us is the massive hardwood staircase that arches upward toward the second floor bedrooms. Everything feels more extravagant and grandiose than the pictures even portrayed. Honestly, they didn't do it justice.

Crap, this was so a crack house.

"Uh, Mom. I hate to be the bearer of bad news, but..." Asher begins, stepping into the open living room space. His voice echoes across the hardwood floors as he spins in a slow circle. "Where's all our stuff?"

The high I was riding comes crashing down around me.

"Yeah, what the heck? Where's our couch and TV?" Avery asks, following her brother.

"Shit," I mutter, walking into the dining room. "Nothing here either."

Together, the three of us ascend the staircase, making our way to the three bedrooms on the upper level. Again, each bedroom is devoid of any sign of life. The entire house is vacant.

"Goddamn moving company," I spit, pulling my cellphone from my pocket.

I punch the number from my recent calls history as I try not to breathe fire from my nostrils. After four and a half rings, the voicemail picks up. "Hello, you've reached Tabula Rasa Moving Company. Our business hours are eight am to five pm Pacific time. If you've reached us after business hours, please call back another time or leave us a voice message. We'll get back to you as soon as we can. BEEP."

"Uh, hi. This is Ella Breene again. I was told our stuff was meant to be delivered to our home in Oregon yesterday and we just arrived to an empty house," I begin.

"Where the hell is our stuff?" Avery blurts out, jumping in close so she can be heard by the machine.

I clutch the microphone part of my phone and shoot her a look of warning to back up. When she stumbles backward, I return to the call. "At any rate, I'm not super thrilled. We're at the house and have no beds to sleep on. Can someone please call me back as soon as possible so I know what to expect here? You have my number. Thanks."

I end the call and sweep my gaze across the empty master bedroom.

"So, what do we do now?" Asher says, crossing his arms. "Do we need to find another hotel room or something?"

I shake my head. "I only budgeted for the five nights. We're gonna have to tough it out here. Do either of you know if the sleeping bags managed to make it with us? Or did they go in the big truck?"

"I have no clue about sleeping bags, but Ash and I have our blankets and pillow, remember?" Avery says, scratching at her temple.

They're like me that way. They can't sleep without a little bit of home with them. Turns out to be a good thing in this case.

I nod. "Yeah, I have my pillow, too. Shit, I hope the sleeping bags made it though. Otherwise, I might have to make a quick trip to Target or something to get us some new ones."

"Wouldn't that cost as much as a hotel room?" Asher says, ever the mature one.

I think on his words a moment and while *technically* true, now that I'm in my actual new house, the last thing I want to do is sleep somewhere else.

"Maybe so. But I'm not going to let a simple inconvenience kick me out of my house. I've had a long ass day and I deserve to be excited and embrace this moment. Warts and all," I say, forcing my chin up.

"Well, I sure as hell hope you brought toilet paper,

because I still gotta take a dump. Gonna go find the bathroom," Asher says, walking out of the master bedroom and into the hallway.

"Boys," Avery mutters under her breath. "Everything's about farts, poop, and burps."

"Don't I know it?" I nod. "Thankfully, I've moved before, so I did come prepared with toilet paper. I'm gonna go root it out of the truck, then run to the store."

With a little less pep in my step, I make my way down the beautiful staircase and out the front door. After digging around the Highlander's jam-packed back end, I locate the four-pack of toilet paper I brought for move-in day and slam the back door shut.

Avery is leaning against the railing of the stairs with her arm crossed when I get to the front. "He's already yelling for toilet paper."

"Good god, give this to him. I'll go grab new sleeping bags and I'll pick up some pizza on the way back," I say, handing her the package.

"Gee, just what I always wanted. To be my brother's toilet paper slave. My role in life is complete," she says, hugging the toilet paper to her chest.

I make a face and point to the front door. "Get inside. I'll be back in a few minutes."

"Aren't you gonna at least change? You've still got blood on your—"

I swipe a hand in the air. "Eh, I'm beyond vanity. Screw it. I just want to get the loot and get back."

Without another word, I turn on my heel and make my way back to the vehicle, tugging my keys from my pocket as I do so.

When life gives you lemons, it's time to squeeze those bad boys out and make some Long Island Ice Teas and enjoy the chaos. I refuse to let this little blimp derail me, dammit.

When I reach the Highlander, the hairs on the back of my neck rise and an intense feeling of being watched rolls through me. I glance up, suddenly more aware of my surroundings.

My voice quivers more than I'd like when I say, "Is someone out here?"

CHAPTER 6
UNDERWEAR GHOST AND OTHER SCARY STORIES

ELLA

I can't pinpoint anything out of the ordinary, at least, nothing that stands out and screams, "Watch out—murderer incoming." Our yard is fenced and there's basically nowhere to hide. Not well, anyway.

Just to be sure, I grab hold of my keys, clutching them between my fingers as I walk the sidewalk to the backyard. The feeling persists, but as I scan the open grass, beautifully tended flowers, and large willow tree in the back, nothing appears out of place there, either.

Yay for new home, new territory nerves.

Rather than worrying anyone, I send a text to both Avery and Asher.

. . .

Make sure the door is locked and call me if you need anything other than the sleeping bags. BRB. Love you!

Clutching the phone in my left hand, I walk to the driver's side door and hop inside. The strange feeling hasn't really subsided, but I shake it off and put the Highlander into reverse.

The trip to the store doesn't take long, since the town isn't super big. Sure, there's the local bar, a coffee shop that looks like it hasn't been updated into the new millennium, a smattering of churches, and of course, the standard box stores like Target and Walmart. Nothing about it overly stands out in a way that screams unique, but it's quaint enough that I could totally see myself living out the rest of my days in the quiet of that big backyard of mine.

Thanks to the magic of smartphones, and my map app, in less than twenty minutes, I've picked out three decent, but cheap, sleeping bags, as well as managed to find a place that does take-n-bake pizzas.

Score.

By the time I get home, the only thing I can think about is how fast the oven will preheat and how I should have called the kids to make them turn it on when I was on my way back.

On the upside, at least the electric company wasn't

as incompetent as my movers, and the pizza was done in no time.

"So, what's the game plan here?" I ask, shoving a drooping bite of gourmet veggie pizza into my mouth.

"What do you mean?" Asher asks, reaching for his fourth slice of pepperoni.

"Are we all gonna go our separate ways and test out our new bedrooms tonight? Or are we gonna pretend we're on a campout and sleep here in the wide-open spaces of the living room?" I ask, suggesting to the large, devoid location surrounding us.

The side of Asher's nose twitches, as if it offends him that I'd even suggest sleeping in the same room again after five nights on the road.

Avery, on the other hand, looks conflicted, but she eyes her brother for her cue. Always the parrot in terms of defying her mom.

"Look, guys, you aren't going to hurt my feelings if you want to sleep in your own room. I get it. Mom's just not that cool anymore," I say, rolling my eyes and really amping up my sarcasm for good measure.

"It's not that—" Asher begins.

I hold out a hand, twisting my nose to the ceiling. "No, no... I get it. Totally fine." I pretend to wipe away a tear from my cheek.

Both kids groan in unison.

On the inside, I grin triumphantly. Outwardly, I clutch at my chest, like my beating heart is about to shatter. "Seriously, I'm a big girl. I can sleep all by own self. *Alone.*"

"For crying out loud," Asher says, running his hand down his face.

"You want us to camp out in the living room, don't you?" Avery asks. It's not really a question, it's more of a statement because she knows me that well.

"Hmmm, now that you bring it up..." I say, turning to face them with a sweet grin. "We could pop popcorn in the microwave and tell ghost stories by the fire."

"We're not actually camping, Mom," Avery mutters.

I jab my index finger toward the fireplace.

"Fine," Asher says, hanging his head in defeat. He always was a smart cookie.

I clap my hands like a seven-year-old kid who was just told it was the Scholastic book fair day. Or maybe it was just me... Either way, totally stoked. It will be a great way to celebrate our first night in the house, and as a bonus, the kids have something fun to look back on. They need more of that in their lives.

"Do I get to light the fire?" Asher asks, setting down his pizza and wiping his hands in front of him.

I thrust my hands out. "Whoa, hold up there, buckeroo. Do you know how to light the fire?"

"It's gas, Mom. How hard can it be?" He shrugs.

Throwing my hands out in acceptance, I bow my head. "Fair enough. Do your worst."

"Mom, do you think this is wise?" Avery asks, panic hidden in her dark brown eyes.

I glance her direction, blinking slowly. I know for a fact that gas fireplaces are a pain in the absolute ass to light and the chances of him getting the thing going this side of my forty-fifth birthday is highly—

"Got it," Asher says, closing the grate on the front with a clang.

I spin around. "What? That's not possible." Yet, sure as shit, soft flames lick at the glass rocks and fake logs stacked in the middle of the fireplace.

"Huh, guess he's useful for something after all," Avery says, leaning back and resting on her hands.

"Shut up," Asher says, resuming his seat. "At least I can do more than record lame videos for TikTok."

Avery's right-hand rears up and I reach between them, shoving them both in opposite directions. "Enough. We have tales to tell," I say, straightening my shoulders. The ambiance from the lit fireplace highlights nicely the setting sun and the darkening of the living room. The whole thing sets the mood perfectly for a spooky fun evening.

I rub my hands together, excited.

Both children stare at me blankly.

My gaze floats to the ceiling. Guess this is on me to start.

"Ye intruders beware..." I begin, wiggling my fingers on either side of my face.

"Mom," the two of them groan.

"Not Goonies again. Seriously, we're way past the haunted pirate phase," Asher announces, rolling his eyes.

"And we've seen the movie like a hundred times. We know where the story comes from, so it's lost all its magic," Avery retorts.

My shoulders slump. "Psh. Fine. You tell a story, then." I jab a finger in Asher's direction. That ought to learn him.

His face crumples, but then an evil grin spreads across his lips.

"Oh no..." Avery says, shaking her head.

"I take it back—" I say.

"There once was an old man who always wore two pairs of underwear..." Asher begins.

Avery makes a face and lowers her eyebrows at me. "See what you unleashed?"

"Quiet. I'm telling the story," Asher says, holding a finger to his lips. "As I was saying... There was an old dude with two pairs of underwear."

"Were they tighty-whities? Or speedos?" Avery interjects.

"Speedos are for swimming," I say, somehow feeling the need to differentiate the two before I can stop myself.

"Whatever." She swipes at the air between us, evidently not fussed.

Asher crosses his arms over his chest.

"Sorry, sorry," I mutter, rolling my hand out in front of me and urging him to continue.

He clears his throat. "The man died suddenly and his wife was beside herself with grief. She took care of everything in a daze. The funeral, the burial..."

"Wow, this is cheery—" Avery mutters.

Asher reaches out, placing his palm over her mouth, and keeps going. "However, after the funeral, the man's wife began seeing his ghost. Every night, he'd haunt her. She got so scared that finally, she moved away, but the man found her no matter where she went. Finally, scared out of her mind, she asked him... 'What do you want? Why won't you leave me alone?'" Avery shoves his hand from her mouth and he clasps them together beneath this chin. "The ghost of the old man stared at his wife a long time, indignant. Finally, he replied, 'Woman, gimme my second pair of underwear.'"

Both Avery and I groan.

Ignoring us, he continues, "So, the old woman dug up her husband's body to find she forgot to bury him with his second pair of underwear. They remedied the situation on his shriveled old—"

"Asher," I warn, quirking an eyebrow.

He clears his throat. "And he was never seen from again."

"Wow, that was..." Avery begins, "the dumbest ghost story ever."

"Shut up. It was epic. Let's see you do better, then,

Miss Prolific," Asher says, shoving Avery in the shoulder.

"Oh, don't you worry, I will," Avery says, dropping her tone into what I can only describe as her mystery voice. "There once was a priest—"

"Don't tell me... He walked into a bar," Asher says, chuckling under his breath.

My right eye twitches. Maybe we should be sleeping in our separate rooms.

"Anyway," she says, sending a side-eye to her brother the way only a sister can, "The priest was on a trip to a neighboring town to do whatever priests do. But the trip was taking forever and it was in the time before cars and shi—stuff." Her bottom lip tugs downward, but she carries on, despite her close call.

"Does this story have a point?" Asher asks, pretending to yawn.

Avery's left-hand whips out and smacks Asher across the side of his torso.

"Guys, seriously. You're not two and five anymore. Come on," I say, letting my head fall back for a moment.

Avery leans in, focusing on me and ignoring her brother now. "Because the journey was on foot, the priest had to stop for the night and set up camp. But little did he know, the forest he set up camp in was totally haunted."

"Ooooh, intrigue," Asher says, bobbling his head on his shoulder.

I shoot him a glare and his mouth snaps shut.

Avery grins, clearly enjoying her brother being reprimanded. "During the night, the priest heard clawing and scratching outside his tent. When he went outside to check it out—"

"If you were in a haunted forest and heard there was scratching outside your tent, why in the hell would you go outside?" Asher says.

"He didn't know it was haunted," Avery says, shaking her head like her brother is dense. "So, he goes outside to find a gigantic wolf—kinda like the one we saw earlier today."

I lean in, placing my elbows on my knees and resting my chin in my steepled hands.

She grins, happy to know she has at least one enraptured listener. "Well, since he was a priest, he didn't have anything to protect himself from the wolf, it attacked. The priest tried to fend off the wolf, but it was too strong. The wolf bit the priest, and just as it was about to tear out the man's throat, it caught sight of the cross around his neck thanks to the moonlight shining down."

"Nice imagery," I say, nodding my head in approval. She definitely has potential as a storyteller.

Instead of accepting the compliment, she looks over her shoulder and sticks out her tongue at her brother.

"Yeah, yeah. Hurry up with it, would you?" Asher says, urging her on with his hand.

"The wolf backed away, staring at the man and the cross. Then, inexplicably, it ran away—leaving the priest lying in a pool of blood and exposed to the elements."

The hairs on the back of my neck stand on end and I shiver away the sudden rise of anxiety.

"How was that inexplicable? I mean, werewolves hate silver, right?" Asher asks.

"No one said anything about werewolves, dummy," Avery spat back.

"I just did," Asher retorts.

Ignoring them both, I whisper conspiratorially. "Oooh, what if it was the cross itself? Maybe they're like vampires and hate the church?"

"Is that a thing?" Avery asks, seriously.

"God, this story is going to go on all night," Asher mumbles.

"Fine, fine," Avery says, shaking her head. "Anyway, the next morning, the priest made his way back to his town. When he got there, he collapsed outside the local doctor's house. A few days later, he woke up to find all of his wounds healed and thanked the doctor profusely for saving his life. The priest went on his merry way, growing his church and making his people happy. But at the next full moon, a small child went missing. Then, a month later, a woman was found butchered outside the town. These weird things continued to happen each month around the time of the full moon."

"See, told you. Werewolf," Asher said, nodding his head.

I nod back, in total agreement with the direction of this story.

Avery again eyes him but doesn't respond. "The priest begins to wonder why God would have cursed his village with all this death and destruction. One night, the villagers decide they've had enough. They band together to capture whoever is behind these horrific events."

"Bet I know who's about to get busted," Asher mumbles.

"Mom, can you make him shut up?" Avery whines.

"Asher, let her finish," I say, casting a knowing look his direction.

He hefts a sigh and grabs another pizza slice. By now, the remaining light has vanished beneath the horizon, and the light of the rising moon crests through the tree branches beyond the window. Again, I shiver, unable to shake away the bizarre déjà vu rumbling through me.

"So, the villagers staged a trap. They tie the biggest dude in the town to a tree and wait for the killer to come upon him," she says.

"Why do I find that hard to believe?" Asher asks.

"Because you're dense. Shut up and listen. It's my story," Avery says through the side of her mouth, refusing to look at her brother. "Well, the town fully anticipated the killer to be a man or someone who would come into the town from time to time. They weren't expecting the enormous wolf that strolled up, ready to feast upon the guy tied to the tree."

"Uh-oh," I say, waiting for the twist I know is coming.

"So," Avery says, continuing to enhance her tone to play up the suspense, "when they see the wolf, they cut the man free and a trap is sprung, capturing the wolf. The villagers attack the caged wolf, jabbing it with long spears until someone manages to pierce its heart. When this happens, everyone jumps back in surprise. There, before their eyes, the wolf begins to transform from a hairy beast into a man."

Avery pauses for effect, finally glancing between me and Asher.

"Go on," I say, wanting to know if I'm right.

"The villagers cried out in dismay, falling to their knees and weeping. They had killed their beloved priest," she says, amping up the ending and dropping her chin to her chest for effect.

"No way. I totally didn't see that coming," Asher says, laying the sarcasm on thick.

"Shut up. It was still better than your underwear ghost," Avery snorts.

I stare out the window toward the nearly full moon and goosebumps flash across my skin. My stomach rolls and I suddenly don't feel very well.

"You know what, guys... Maybe we should sleep in

our rooms," I say, grabbing my paper plate and collecting the now empty cardboard pizza trays.

"What? I thought you wanted to stay up telling scary stories?" Avery says, frowning.

"I know. I'm just..." I clutch my stomach, wondering if the pizzas weren't such a good idea after all. "I'm feeling kinda yucky. Too much pizza or something. I'm gonna go sleep it off and hope I don't give it to you."

"Mom, do you think it has anything to do with today?" Asher asks, his face serious.

"What do you mean?"

He shrugs. "I mean, after the accident, you probably should have gotten checked out. What if that guy had some sort of virus or something."

"Ooooh, what if he was a werewolf," Avery says, dancing her fingers out in front of her.

"You're ridiculous, you know that, right?" Asher says, making a face. "Werewolves aren't real."

"How do you know?" she asks, jogging her head from side to side.

"Night, Mom," Asher says, ignoring her. Instead, he stands up, reaching out and wrapping his arms around me. I return the embrace, then turn and do the same for Avery.

"Night guys," I say, ruffling Asher's hair. "Love you both."

"See you in the morning, Mom," Avery says, a soft

smile lighting up her face. It's so good to see them both happy.

Despite feeling totally off, I can't help but smile back.

I make my way to the kitchen, dumping the garbage on the counter to deal with in the morning. Then, I make my way upstairs, placing out the sleeping bag and scooting inside. It won't be the best night of sleep ever, but at least I have my own pillow.

My stomach constricts again and I swallow hard, hoping the pizza isn't trying to find a way to come back up. Absently, I itch at my left arm, my fingernails grazing the spot where the bite marks should be. While I know werewolves aren't real, the day's events leave me wondering if there were ever truths hidden in the lore.

Maybe Asher is right. I should have at least stopped at the clinic to get my arm checked out.

Something to add to the list for tomorrow.

CHAPTER 7
HOT MESS EXPRESS
ELLA

Those dark, stormy emerald eyes...

For the briefest of moments, I swear they turn golden, sparking in the center of his iris like a firecracker exploding to life.

I could very easily get lost in him. Those eyes, his strong arms, and chiseled upper body...

I shudder away the desire that rolls through me as he inches himself closer. His warm breath caresses my cheek, instantly causing goosebumps to erupt across my skin. My breath hitches and I watch him, mesmerized by the way he moves and the glinting gold in his otherwise green eyes.

Before I realize what he's doing, he places his lips against the hollow of my throat. I lean back, giving him access, allowing him to burn his kisses along my neck and anywhere else he'd like to.

All too soon, he pulls back, a slow, half-smile

gracing his beautiful lips. God, I would give him all of me. All he'd have to do is say the word and my soul would crack open and bleed for him.

My heartbeat quickens and I lick my lower lip in anticipation of what he might do next. This is everything I ever wanted...

I close my eyes, needing to experience the tactile feeling of his touch as vividly as I can.

The sensation that greets me is nothing like I anticipated. Instead, of the pleasure of his mouth and hands, his teeth clamp down on my throat. My eyes pop open as he rips open my jugular with a quick jerk.

Blood gushes from the wound, splattering across his face and closing off my airway. Almost immediately, my body convulses as the most intense pain I've ever felt erupts through me like a lightning bolt.

I reach out, clawing at his face, trying to pry the weight of his body off of me. But the more I fight, the more the room spins and my energy wanes.

Darkness gropes for me and my eyes flitter closed.

I bolt upright in bed, clutching at my throat.

Despite my body's utter protest to sleeping on the floor, the only thing I can do is sit there, letting the feelings wash over me again and again.

For the longest time, I stare at the blank wall in front of me, unable to see anything but the horror left in the dream's wake. Breathing deeply, I will my heart to stop bursting out of my chest.

Everything about it felt so real. There was a closeness there—a deep desire and need for a man and I don't even know his name.

Christ, what was that all about?

And then there was the violence. In all my life, I've never had a dream like that.

Evidently, the scary story Avery told last night got to me. That's the only explanation. Granted, I'm sure getting bitten by the dying man yesterday was in there, too. My brain is trying to process it all.

I run my right hand over my left bicep, feeling where the bite marks should be. While the man bit my arm and not my neck, the absolute terror in the moment was the same.

And all the blood...

I shake my head, unable to believe the gory mess was really coming from him. I could have sworn it was from me.

Then, of course, the hot guy in the ravine didn't help my weird dreamscape situation, either, since he was the main attraction of that shit show nightmare.

Seriously, no man should be that sculpted. It's not natural. So, of course, I'd find a way to make him a baddie.

I try to ignore the tendrils from the lust-filled fantasy before it all went sideways. Despite being killed in my dream, part of me is deeply saddened our connection wasn't real. It's like a piece of my soul was ripped away and now I'm lost.

Goodness knows it's been a long damn time since I got laid, but I need to get a grip. Dreaming about the first guy I happen to come across who's in the relative age range I am is a bit on the weird side. And feeling so...*saddened* by it not being real is beyond strange.

Besides, he could be married for all I know... Granted, I didn't see a ring.

I sigh, kicking myself out of the sleeping bag and standing up. I need to move around; ground myself in reality a bit. Throwing on my mandala sweatpants, I pad my way to the bathroom.

Why did he have to have tattoos? He was practically a billboard screaming 'bad boy' and despite myself, I can't help but be intrigued.

Goddammit.

When I decided to get a divorce, I'd made a pact with myself that I'd give up on men. Especially ones that would be a thorn in my side and make me regret my decisions. He would certainly be one of those.

No, I made up my mind. I need to rediscover myself, not fall into the orbit of the first guy I meet. That is the damn priority here.

After doing my business, I press my hands against the sink and I stare at my reflection in the bathroom mirror. Despite myself, I narrow my gaze the way I would to Avery or Asher when I need to drive home a point.

"Don't you even think about it," I say, jabbing my index finger toward the mirror. "You've got big things to do with your life."

Nodding to myself, I exit the bathroom and head downstairs to scrounge for coffee. My back continues to ache and I'm fairly certain I have a permanent kink in my neck now.

God, I hope the movers come today. I could really use a good night's sleep in my own bed.

When I get downstairs, I'm surprised to see both Avery and Asher awake and belly up to the breakfast bar with their phones in their hands, but for once, not arguing.

"Do you think this is the guy?" Avery asks, leaning over to show her brother something on the screen.

"Looks like the car," he responds.

"What are you guys looking at?" I ask, crowding in between them.

Avery squeals and nearly drops her phone, evidently not expecting me.

I chuckle, shaking my head. Looks like I'm not the only one who could use a good night's sleep.

"We were just checking to see if the crash was in the news," Asher says, sliding off his stool and making his way to the fridge. He grabs a can of soda and offers one out to me.

I thrust out my hands and shake my head. "No, thank you. I need something stronger than high fructose corn syrup."

He shrugs, silently offering the other can to Avery, who snatches it up, no questions asked.

"How'd you sleep?" Asher asks, resuming his spot at the breakfast bar.

I walk to the fridge and open it in the hopes that coffee magically appeared in there overnight. I'd even take the disgusting cold coffee at this point. But alas, it's as bare as it was before.

I really should have thought through the morning wake-up when I got pizza last night.

Sighing to myself, I close the fridge door and turn on my heel. "I'm gonna head to the coffee shop."

"Where's that?" Avery asks, spinning around on her stool as I walk by.

"No clue, but I'm an adult and I'll follow my internal compass guiding me to caffeine," I say, leaving the kitchen and making my way back to the stairs. I need shoes and a bra if I plan to go out in public.

"Can I come with?" Avery asks, following after me.

I groan, dropping my chin to my chest. "Honey, as much as I love you—and I really do—Mom needs caffeine before she can deal with tween talking."

She sticks her lower lip out and pouts.

I quirk an eyebrow. "If you stay here with Asher, I'll pick you both up something, though."

Her face instantly brightens and she spins on her heel. "Okay."

I blow out a puff of air. "Narrowly dodged that

bullet," I mutter under my breath as I walk into my bedroom.

I slide my feet into my sandals, which will have to do because I can't be bothered to find socks and tie laces. In fact, scratch the bra, too. Most coffee places have drive-thrus now. Besides, if anyone has a problem with how I'm dressed, they shouldn't be staring at a middle-aged woman's boobs, anyway.

I'm not going out to impress anyone. I'm going to get coffee, dammit. I'm too old for vanity.

Trudging down the stairs with cellphone in hand, I pick up my keys, and head out the door.

"Be right back," I call out, closing the door behind me before anyone can protest or give me their wish list. The only thing I want to worry about is how close the coffee shop is, how much caffeine is too much, and please god, please... let there be a drive-thru.

When I get in the vehicle, I ask Siri where the nearest coffee shop is and start driving based on his recommendation. The British voice directs my turns; the closest thing I can get to having Jarvis as my AI.

Thankfully, getting to the coffee shop only takes six minutes. Unfortunately, because of the proximity to the hospital, the location appears to be a hub for everyone who either works there, or is planning to visit. People go in and out like bees visiting their hive.

"Shit," I breathe, slipping into a recently vacated parking spot and cutting the engine.

Either I continue to drive around in the hopes of

finding a coffee shop with a drive-thru, or I suck it up, own my middle-aged madness, and get some mother-fucking coffee.

"Shit," I repeat, grabbing my purse and exiting the vehicle.

I hold my head up high, making my way inside the coffee shop like I own the place, despite feeling that I should have taken Avery up on her offer to come with. I could have sent her in to get the drinks instead.

Mental note taken.

I look around, acutely aware that everyone in this joint is well-dressed. Either doctors, nurses, or just plain wanting to impress, I stand out like a sore thumb.

Not only do I have crazy curly dark hair that probably should have been brushed and put into a mom-bun, but I don't have an ounce of makeup on. Add in the lack of a bra and I'm basically announcing to the world that I'm a gigantic hot mess. Fan-fucking-tastic.

"Can I help you?" the barista asks. His hair is a bright teal and the dark eyeliner and painted nails scream non-binary, even if his voice and stance didn't do it for him.

"Hey," I say, putting on my most secure, 'own the day attitude.' "I need the world's largest light roast coffee, black like my soul."

The guy chuckles, instantly endearing me to him.

"Then I guess I need two medium matcha tea cooler things," I continue.

"Bubbles or no bubbles?" he asks, smirking slightly.

I lean in. "What in the actual hell are bubbles? Is that like carbonated tea? Or—?"

Again he laughs. "No, they're basically like Orbeez but you can eat 'em."

The simple fact that he was secure in knowing I'd have a clue what Orbeez were means my hot mess mom vibe is going strong. Asher couldn't get enough of them as a kid.

"Ah...okay. So, teens like that sorta thing?" I ask.

He grins. "They're pretty popular, yeah."

I wave in acceptance of his recommendation. "Fair enough. Bring on the bubbles."

He nods. "You got it. Anything else?"

"What are you doing here?"

I look over my shoulder, only half-listening, but double-take when I realize I'm staring into the emerald eyes of the guy from yesterday. He's clad in light blue denim, with a dark purple dress shirt tucked in, with his sleeves rolled up to his elbows, showing a hint of his tattoos across his forearms. If I thought he was hot before, this adds a whole different dimension for my imagination to play with.

Heat creeps into my cheeks as the memory of the dream slams into me. But then, I remember how it ended. And how I'm currently dressed.

Since running doesn't seem like a valid option, I slide into snarkasm, hoping to deflect.

One of my eyebrows rises of its own accord and I point to the barista in way of my explanation. Because using my voice might result in it squeaking and it would ruin my vibe.

"Hey, Stone. How's it going, man?" The barista says, tipping his chin toward the muscle man.

Stone?

Like, is that his name? Or was he poking fun of the amount of muscle the guy carries around on him? Until I get confirmation, I'll go with the latter.

"Good, thanks, Jason. How's your mom?" Sexy, obnoxious muscle man asks.

"Better," the teal-haired barista says, beaming. "We appreciate your help."

"Good," muscle man says, returning his piercing green eyes to me.

I clear my throat, trying to sound more in control than I feel. "So, what are you doing here?"

Tall, dark, and tanned stares at me for a moment, his eyelashes fluttering against his cheeks. "Well, I work at the hospital, so..."

I tip my chin in acknowledgment. "Ohhhh."

Well, that makes a certain amount of sense.

Suddenly, I catch a whiff of his cologne and my pulse rate quickens. God, he smells good, too. Could this be any worse?

"Sorry, ma'am. Was there anything else to add?" The barista asks again, trying to be cordial.

I shake my head, stumbling out of the way, as I head to the retrieval counter.

"Stone, did I hear things right? Alph—er," a smartly dressed man with a bald head asks, walking up from the depths of the dining area. "Douglas is gone?"

Evidently, Stone it is.

He nods solemnly.

"Shit, man. I'm sorry. I know you two weren't close lately, but—"

He waves off the man's words. "Water under the bridge. I'm more concerned about who did it."

The other man nods.

"Well, I better..." Stone says, pointing at Jason the barista.

"Yeah, sorry. We can talk later." The other guy nods to himself and walks off.

I narrow my gaze, confused by the entire exchange. If Douglas is Stone's brother-in-law, it's odd that the other guy didn't even question what Stone meant. Instead, it's like he takes Stone's words at face value— like he knew he was driven off the road. Then again, it's not that big of a town.

Stone orders, then follows over to the waiting area where I stand.

I plant my gaze along the wall, pretending to read the notes patrons have left on the chalkboard meant for customer engagement. But I can't help but inhale deeply, trying to simultaneously enjoy and ignore the way my body reacts to having him nearby.

"Don't you think you should actually get dressed before going out in public?" Stone asks, glancing over his shoulder like he's afraid to be seen with me.

With those simple words, my high comes crashing down.

"Large light-roast," the barista making my coffee says, passing it across the counter.

My face burns and I grab the cup, spinning on my heel and walking out. It's not until I reach the safety of my Highlander that I realize I forgot the rest of my order.

Mortified, I drop my forehead to the center of the steering wheel, making it honk and scaring the shit of out me.

Maybe moving to Oregon wasn't my smartest idea ever.

CHAPTER 8
THE OMEGA
STONE

Stone watched, entranced, as Ella snatched her beverage from the barista and raced from the coffee shop. He chuckled under his breath, unable to help himself. Her face had turned a bright fuchsia, adding some much-needed color to her cheeks.

He had to admit, being in her presence for the second time was just as heady as it was the first. It was like everything inside him was lighter—*and vibrating.*

What was up with that?

As thrilling as that was, it was even better when he realized he had a similar effect on her. He could sense that, too. It was evident in the way her pulse quickened and the way her body moved when she pretended to ignore him. She moved like she was craving something from him, even though she didn't know what. Or why.

Whatever Doug had done to her, *and he hoped it wasn't what he thought it was,* it was messing with his head—and more than a bit with his body. There was a strange pull, like a cord being yanked straight from the middle of his torso, and it worsened whenever she was out of his sight.

He'd spent the better part of yesterday, following her, learning where she lived, who she was with, and what kind of person she was. If she was about to become what he feared she might...he needed answers.

He now knew she was a mom of two teens. One boy, one girl. She'd just moved to town and bought the old St. Patrick house—which he also knew was barren, thanks to the mover's ineptitude, apparently.

He also knew her name was Ella Breene, aged 42.

The one thing he didn't know was whether or not the kids' father would be making a later appearance. He kinda hoped not.

There was a lot he'd learned in a short period of time. But he was still shouldering a bit of guilt.

Stone *should have* been mourning the loss of his brother-in-law with the rest of his pack. But deep down, he knew his time was better spent in recon.

Doug might have been Alpha, but Stone was the outsider. The castaway.

Their Omega.

He was only accepted by some because of his sister. He knew that just as well as anybody.

Most days, it was fine by him. He didn't like the majority of them anyway.

That wasn't true. He loved Doug like the brother he was. And most of the pack had their endearing qualities. It was really just Silas who could go to hell. Silas and his gang.

The pack's Beta had made it very clear, in no uncertain terms, that Stone wasn't wanted. Hell, he went out of his way to prove that fact and it was no secret the two of them didn't think very highly of each other.

For the sake of his sister, Stone kept his distance, watching and learning in a way that no insider would ever be privy to. He considered it his superpower because he could see and hear all just by blending into the background.

It's how he knew Silas was up to something. And even though he was right, he hated to admit it— because look where it got them. Doug had refused to remove Silas as Beta and Stone was pretty sure that backstabbing bastard was the reason for his demise.

He'd been a hair too slow to witness the crash, thanks to noticing Ella's vehicle when he was in wolf form. The Highlander didn't smell right. Definitely not from around here—and he had stop to catch a glimpse of her as she drove by. He had reasoned it was in case he'd need the information later on.

Turns out he had, only not because of what he had originally wondered. Oh no, it was far worse.

Now, with Doug out of the way, there's nothing keeping Silas from taking over the Alpha role. Unless, of course, Doug passed the baton to someone else.

Stone narrowed his eyes, waiting for the Highlander to back up and move on. But it didn't.

He drummed his fingertips on the outside of his cup, waiting. He felt protective of the woman and was drawn to her in ways he could only speculate.

If Doug had listened—if he had noticed the way Silas was behaving, maybe in his final moments he chose to act. And if he had...well, that would be a monumentally big deal.

It would either be a colossal mistake. Or the saving grace for the Black Crater Pack.

Stone grabbed his coffee and walked over to the window to watch her leave, whenever that might be. Instead, her horn honked and she let out a squeal inside the vehicle, evidently having startled herself.

Again, he laughed, then took a swig of his coffee.

It had been a while since he last felt so...*light*. Without a mate, and without a pack, his life wasn't necessarily the stuff of legends. For a moment, he wondered if Ella had something to do with this lightness. It would make sense if Doug had passed on his birthright.

Stone took a moment and honed his senses, perking his ears, and listening to see if she'd say anything out loud. If Douglas had bitten her, he'd know soon enough. Her thoughts and feelings would start to bubble to the surface and he'd be able to connect to her mind. At least, until she learned how to control it. Then, only her chosen mate would have access to her thoughts and feelings. She, on the other hand, would be able to hear and sense everyone at a moment's notice.

The blessing and curse of an Alpha.

When Ella didn't say anything, and didn't leave the lot, Stone moved to a window table and took a seat. There was obviously a reason she was still here, and he was just as keen to learn what it was. Besides, he'd only be following her back to her place to keep watch.

A moment later, Ella's driver's side door opened and she huffed her way back inside the coffee shop. Stone smiled to himself and took another sip of coffee, watching her struggle with her embarrassment and determination.

She'd forgotten something, and she clearly wasn't going to leave it behind.

When she entered the shop, she deliberately threw her shoulders back and thrust her chin up. Her dark brown hair was as wild as her tenacity, and he briefly wondered what she'd look like if she put a little more effort into her appearance. Not that she needed it. There was a wild, untamed beauty about her that was evident. It was like she knew she was beautiful, and didn't need anyone else to tell her so. He respected that.

Her dark brown eyes caught his when her gaze swept the coffee shop. A jolt of energy coursed through his midsection, making its way to his groin. He tilted his head slightly, took another sip, and adjusted in his seat.

"Ah, yeah, hi—" she said, leaning in closer to the barista at the end of the pick-up line. "I forgot some of my order. They're some green bubble things?"

"Oh, yeah. I was wondering if you were gonna come back. They got a little melty. Let me make them over for you quick." The guy flashed her a smile, before turning back to the machines behind him.

"Oh, thank you. I really appreciate that," she said, her tone painted by embarrassment and relief.

For a moment, she spun around, again locking eyes with Stone. Her lips parted, like she was about to say something, only she was too far to strike up a conversation with him. At least to her knowledge.

But before he could do anything, not that he had any idea what, the barista handed her the two green drinks. She passed over a tip, then grabbed the drinks from him. Without another glance toward Stone's direction, she marched out of the coffee shop and back to her vehicle.

Despite himself, Stone's gaze roamed to her swaying backside. Even in a pair of sweatpants, which ordinarily hid a figure well, his imagination began running scenarios.

Again, he shifted in his seat, adjusting himself. He shook his head, practically growling into his cup.

"Christ, Stone. Get it together. She could be your —" His lips clamped down and his gaze slid sideways.

He was surrounded by other wolves from the pack. All with the same supernatural hearing he had.

And if they knew—or suspected what he did— they'd be on the hunt for her.

Some to help her. Some to put an end to her. Some wanting to bed her to be the mate to the first female Alpha in centuries.

He knew which end of the spectrum he fell on, but it was one he could never act on.

Not as the Omega.

So for now, he'd have to settle on keeping tabs and guiding her, should the full moon bring out her inner animal.

His gaze strayed out to the Highlander, now in motion. Stone rose, ready to follow.

Good thing he won't have to wait long to find out if his hunch is correct.

The full moon was only two days away.

What's the worst that could happen? I find out I still don't like runs? Big deal.

Besides, going for a run would allow me to get a better lay of the land...

Good lord, why is everything coming out an innuendo.

Just roll with it.

I pull into my driveway, fully aware that I must be out of my damn mind. First thinking about Stone like he's a slab of meat—*hunky, hunky meat*—then this idea of a run. Nothing about me is normal today.

I shake my head and put the Highlander into park. Before I even get my door open, Avery is outside and bounding down the steps.

"What did you get me?" she asks, practically twirling on the sidewalk. She never was one to wait for surprises.

Without responding, I reach into the vehicle, then hand her both of the green drinks.

A bright smile lights up her face. She takes them without asking who the second one is for, eyes them both, then takes a sip from the one with more bubbles on the bottom. She grins again and spins on her heel. "Thanks, Mom."

I raise my hand to no-one in particular, since she's long gone. "Welcome," I mutter under my breath.

Resting back into my seat, I reach for my coffee and take a sip. The entire way home, I'd been so preoccupied with what happened at the coffee shop, that I hadn't even drank a single drop. Now, I'm regretting that lack of action, because the coffee is lukewarm. *Shit.*

Still clutching the coffee, I close my eyes and thunk my head back on the head rest.

For a few minutes, I rest there, trying to clear my mind.

I exhale sharply. "Fuck it. I'm gonna go for a run. This morning can't get much worse. Can it?" I open my eyes, swap the coffee to my left hand, and grab my purse, so I can follow after Avery.

I have no idea if I have workout clothes packed in my suitcase, but if not, I have a t-shirt and a pair of sleep shorts with my name on them. With a little luck, I'll even have a bra in there somewhere, too.

The last thought makes me huff a laugh and I nearly trip up the front steps because of it. I catch myself like an ungraceful rhino and glance over my shoulder. Thankfully, no one is around to witness it.

I roll my eyes, still mortified by the interaction with Stone.

When I get inside, I march my way upstairs like the woman on a mission I am. Both kids are in their bedrooms, sprawled out on the floor with their drinks within reach and their faces buried in their phones. By the looks of it, they're watching the same Youtube videos. I wonder if they'd be appalled to know that. Smirking to myself, I make my way to my bedroom to hunt for clothes.

After closing the bedroom door, I plant my semi-warm coffee on the window sill and unzip my suitcase. I dig through the entire thing, and the only outfit suitable to run in is a tank top and the sweatpants I'm already wearing. I can't say running with sweats is ideal, since I can't put my phone in my pocket without it being more annoying than the kids fighting, but whatever. On the upside, I found a sports bra in there, so all in all, I consider it a win.

I throw on the workout garb and slam the contents of my coffee. As much as I hate cold coffee, I hate wasting it more. That would be sacrilegious.

With my empty cup in hand, I walk out, feeling the mounting pressure—or persistence of this urge to run.

Embrace it. It's the future you.

I smile to myself. Hell, yes. I could be one of those fit, single moms everyone's always talking about at school gatherings. Maybe that's the new identity I need to embrace.

New town, fresh start. Right?

They don't need to know I'd rather sit on the couch rewatching episodes of *Supernatural* with a pint of Ben & Jerry's.

"Where are you going now?" Avery asks, glancing up at me from the middle of her carpet.

"I'm going for a run," I say, confidently. No time like the present to start the new me.

Avery stares at me like I just said I plan to leave planet Earth to colonize Mars.

"What are you doing?" Asher asks, popping his head out of his bedroom door. In his left hand is his phone, in the right, his nearly empty green drink.

"She's going *running*," Avery answers, adding in air quotes for effect, as she comes out of her bedroom and joins me on the landing.

The two of them exchange a significant glance, evidently silently questioning whether or not I was body snatched.

"Guys, it's not that big of a deal. I just don't like being cooped up in the house without furniture and stuff. I still haven't heard from the movers and rather than get pissy about that fact, I figured I'd get some exercise and stretch my legs. Besides, I want to see more of the town," I say, trying to sound like this is a totally normal thing. "You're more than welcome to come with..."

"No thanks," Asher says, disappearing before the last word has left his lips. He's clearly not worried enough about my sanity to keep me company.

"Nope," Avery parrots, passing me by and taking off down the stairs.

I'm left standing on the landing like a dope. Sighing, I say, "I'll take that as a no, then?"

I jog down the stairs after Avery. Only, rather than heading toward the kitchen like she did, I head for the front door. "I'll be back in a little bit. Don't forget to—"

"Lock the front door. We know," Avery calls out from the kitchen.

I nod. Only she can't see the gesture. Then I stare down at my hand.

Damn cup and no garbage.

"Eh, there are garbages along the way," I mutter, walking out the front door. The June weather is warm, but not so hot that you'd turn right back around rather than run. It would have been that way in California.

I inhale deeply. The scents of cut grass, flowers, and lake fill the air and for whatever reason, it calms me. Like I'm finally *home*. I've never felt like that before. Not in all the years I was married. Hell, not really even before then.

The last time it felt close, was when I was a kid and my parents were still together. That was a long, *long* time ago.

Shaking off that thought, I make my way to the running trail. I start off slow, working myself up from a brisk walk to a jog. It's not like I'm a spry chicken, after all. The last thing I need to do is pull something and have to limp my way home.

I think I've had enough demoralization for the day, thanks.

It doesn't take me long to reach the first neighborhood garbage bin along the trail. I chuck my empty paper cup and take it as a sign to finally put a little speed behind my jaunt. As expected, though, my phone is obnoxious in my pocket, so I pull it out and grip it tightly in my left hand.

For the next few minutes, I find my groove. Despite not having run for decades, it feels good to stretch my legs and work my muscles.

That's it. Go faster.

I pick up speed, racing ahead quicker than I would have thought I could handle at my age. Instead of questioning it, I go with it, focusing on the way my body feels. It's like it's been *waiting* for this.

Before I realize it, I've run for a half hour. I have no idea how far from home that puts me, but I do know, I'm going to need to find a restroom soon. That coffee is catching up to me.

Thanks, tiny Mom bladder.

Who's idea was this anyway? I mean, wow...

Not only do I need to pee, but I can feel the boob sweat building up and droplets making their way down my backside. *Fuck me.*

After years of being uncomfortable, I've decided to let that shit go. Comfort for the win.

Which means next time I get the brilliant idea to run, I'm wearing the right materials that can wick away sweat because this is irritating.

We need to find her.

Startled, I look over my shoulder, expecting to find someone on the phone or running with someone coming up behind me. But I'm the only person within three-block radius.

My speed falters and I slow down.

So, that was weird.

The events from the day before make their way to the forefront of my mind, and I realize I must have been reminding myself about finding the dying man's wife. What was her name again?

Oh, that's right... *Clementine.*

Yes, I do need to find her. I don't care that Stone said he'd pass the message on to his sister. I feel like I need to do it. Like, it was a soul mission or something. I guess the final wish of a dying man sticks with a person.

Hardening my resolve, I promise myself to do some digging when I get back home. I pick up the pace, planning to only go a few more minutes before turning around. I just wanna find a restroom first and I'm almost positive I can see a park from here.

A few more uncomfortable minutes of boob and back sweat and I'm finally within the vicinity of the park. Thank god, I can see a public restroom in the building up ahead, too. Even though it's a part of the lakeside park, it's clearly meant for the dual purpose of relieving those on the trail as well, since a meandering sidewalk veers off to the left.

It's like they know me.

I chuckle to myself as I maintain my jog.

He'll pay. I'll make sure of it.

Wow, I'm all over the place this morning. I shake my head, not quite sure where that thought came from. I mean, I can't say I'm fond of the ex, but I'd say I got the better end of the divorce, since I got the kids. I mean, could be worse. And now I only have to deal with his passive aggressive texts, not his obnoxious face.

It's so weird the way your subconscious can bring up thoughts like that when your guard is down.

Quickening my pace, and beelining for the bathroom, I pass a woman sitting on a park bench overlooking the lake. For some reason, I stop running and glance over my shoulder. The woman is eerily familiar and it isn't until she looks up at me with curious eyes that it clicks into place.

Those green eyes—*they're just like Stone's.*

My heart hammers loudly in my chest as I walk toward her. "I'm sorry, I don't mean to be a total creeper, but...is your name Clementine?"

CHAPTER 10
PROMISE KEPT

ELLA

The woman's eyes flit through a variety of emotions before she finally sputters, "Do I...*know you?*"

Something inside me rises to the surface—like a knowing beyond my typical perception. Even without her confirming, I know without a doubt this is the woman I was meant to find.

I eye the restroom longingly but make my way back to her. "No, my name is Ella. Ella Breene," I say, holding out a hand.

She accepts it, giving it a strong shake.

I pull my hand back, my fingers contorting slightly from the pressure. Woman's got mad strength.

Pressing my fingers against my thighs to stretch them back out, I say, "Are you doing okay?"

She doesn't know me from Jane, and I don't know her, but I can't help but feel for the poor woman. She was obviously adored. I mean, her husband's dying words were to let her know he loved her.

Pretty sure my ex would have wanted someone to tell me to go to hell. Or maybe he wouldn't have even thought about me at all.

Clementine's green eyes glass over. The wind kicks up, tousling her curly brown hair and she tucks a flyaway behind her ear. She swallows hard but doesn't answer.

I take a seat on the bench beside her and place a hand on her knee. I'm not normally a touchy-feely type, but for some reason, the act feels right. "I'm glad I found you. To be honest, I wasn't sure I'd be able. I'm new to town, so this whole thing feels a bit," I glance up into her questioning gaze and clear my throat, then add, *"overwhelming."*

"I'm sorry, I'm not really following," she says, suspicion and concern written in her frown lines.

"Look, I know this probably seems a bit odd, but I" —I lower my voice as I search for the right words—"I was with your husband at the end."

The lightbulb goes off behind Clementine's eyes and she turns to me, grabbing hold of my hand still resting on her knee. "You were with Doug? Was he —?" She shakes her head. "No, I don't want to know." For the first time, her true emotions make their appearance as a tear escapes, blazing a trail down her cheek.

I place my other hand over the top of hers, trying

to comfort her in this impossible position. "He loved you very much. He asked me—"

Clementine's head again jerks up and her gaze deepens as she waits for me to continue.

I inhale deeply, letting my shoulders rise and fall. "He asked me to relay a message to you. He wanted you to know he loved you very much. You were the last thing on his mind before..." My voice trails off and I let things sit there. No need to twist that knife in deeper.

Surprisingly, she huffs a little laugh. "It's just like him to be on his deathbed and only care about getting a message to me. Stupid bastard."

Her words hold admiration, despite their harshness.

I smile softly. "You must have been very important to him."

Her gaze drifts up and out, again resting on the glistening surface of the lake. "He was too caring."

Despite myself, I snicker. "Is there such a thing?"

She shoots me a sideways glance. "Sometimes."

I think about all of the times I tried to make things work with the ex and I know her words hold truth. Sometimes trying to make things right, or caring too much, isn't the right move.

"Fair enough," I say, allowing my gaze to follow hers. The water glitters under the sunlight, pulling away my thoughts. I can see why she chose this spot to sit at today.

"Do you have a husband?" Clementine asks,

turning to me. It's almost as if she was reading my mind.

I shake my head. "No, no husband, thank god. Blissfully single."

"You say that as if you've had experience," she says, the edges of her lips curving upward. Though the emotion doesn't quite make it to her eyes.

I nod. "I was married for a good long while. Too long, if you ask me."

"But it didn't work out?"

"No. If you listen to him tell the story, it's because I didn't know how to be a wife. But really, I reached my bullshit threshold." I shrug, finally returning my hands to my lap.

"I'm sorry. That sounds like a lonely existence," she says, her voice low and soft. Again, something inside me stirs—a deep longing to belong.

It would almost be funny to have her comforting me if the whole situation wasn't so damn sad. Maybe it wasn't just her husband who cared too much.

I inhale sharply through my nose and nod.

"Well, you're still young. There's still plenty of time for fate to intervene," she says, a faint twinkle in her eyes. By the looks of things, she couldn't be much older than I am.

Snickering, I shake my head. "Oh, you've got me all wrong. I'm practically knocking on death's door. Or, at least, that's what my bladder says after that run."

She huffs out a laugh.

"But thank you for the sentiment. In all honesty, I think I'm kinda over guys at this point. I'm thinking of starting a long-term relationship with a box of wine and a good book, though."

Again she laughs. "You're funny. I get why he likes you."

I turn to her, surprised. "Excuse me?"

Biting her lip, she shakes her head slightly. "I meant, liked you. My husband, that is."

"Oh, right." I nod. "I don't think he liked me so much as I was the only person around at the time. He had a message to relay. Remember?"

Clementine narrows her eyes and purses her lips to the side. "No, that wasn't it. There's something about you. I can feel it."

"Oookay, well, I don't know about all of that." My gaze drifts out to the restroom and I stand up. Now feels like a good time to slip away. I can only handle so much weird for one day. I jab a finger toward the public facilities. "I better, get going. Small bladder and all that."

She grins, tipping her chin. "Go. And thanks for stopping, Ella. It was nice to meet you."

"Yeah, I just wish it were under better circum-stances," I say, feeling like an ass for wanting to make a fast getaway. I take a couple of steps away, waving my hand like a kid.

"That makes two of us," she says. "But regardless, we're stuck with each other now."

It's my turn to narrow my eyes. I'm not sure if that was a promise, a threat, or the ramblings of a grieving widow. Either way, I can't help but feel a wave of excitement—like finding my place in this world.

"Mmmkay," I mutter, turning on my heel, and making my way to the bathroom as quickly as my feet will carry me without looking like I'm making a mad dash.

By the time I finish up and exit the building, Clementine is no longer sitting on the bench, thank god. I don't know if I could handle any more awkward conversations.

Honestly, I'm not even sure I heard some of what she said right. Either way, I've done my bit and now I'm ready for a blissfully normal life. That starts, hopefully, with the damn moving company delivering all of our stuff.

I check my watch and start speed-walking toward the trail. It's nearly 11:00 a.m. and I'll need to be ready to place a rage-call if the movers aren't there by the time I get back. When I get to the trail, I shift into a run.

The itch to run is still there, but it's nearly scratched.

Why in the hell did I run so far? What a dunce.

I just know I'm gonna regret it tomorrow, too, when I can't walk straight.

Despite all of that, I continue to huff my way home,

running faster than I ever used to—and probably faster than is wise, considering my years of nonexistent exercise. However, once I get into a good groove, I can't help but love the exertion of it. My muscles feel...*alive.*

When I get home, my body is covered in sweat, but I definitely feel better. Almost happy.

Then, of course, I reach for the door handle to my front door to find it still locked. It's a good thing, but I don't have a key, and now I need to pee again.

I pound on the door, praying one of the kids doesn't have their headphones on, and can actually hear me. Inhaling through my nose, I stare at the door and count to fifty. When nothing happens, I pound again, but reach for my phone, knowing full well they'll need a text intervention.

I quickly type out a message and send it to both kids.

Open the damn door.

Less than a minute later, the door swings open. Asher stands beside the door like an apprentice butler as Avery meanders down the steps without a care in the world.

"Don't everybody race to open the door, or anything," I say, walking inside, once again annoyed.

"I was watching Youtube," Asher says, as if that's a valid explanation for taking ages to come downstairs.

Avery shrugs. "I was in the middle of filming."

"Filming? You mean making fish faces at the camera and trying to find the 'right light' so your face doesn't look like you were swallowed by a ghost," Asher mutters, rolling his eyes and making air quotes.

"Shut up," Avery says, squaring up with her brother.

I get between the two of them. "Enough. Have either of you seen the movers?"

"Does it look like it?" Asher says, quirking an eyebrow and opening his arms wide.

"Fuck," I mutter, again pulling my phone out and dialing the number to the moving company. I step back outside onto the porch, clutching the phone to my head.

After two rings, they pick up.

"Yeah, hi. This is Ella Breene. I called yesterday. We're still waiting for—" I say, before getting cut off.

"The movers are running behind, Ms. Breene," the voice on the other end says. It's the same run around I got yesterday and the way she says Ms. grates my nerves the wrong way.

"Yeah, I know, but I was told our stuff would be here two days ago," I say, anger boiling in my blood. "We need our beds and stuff. This is ridiculous. I—"

Two large moving trucks pull into my driveway and I sigh.

"Nevermind, they just turned up," I mutter, hanging up the phone.

Relief and agitation are a potent mix, but I try to remind myself that it will be nice to sleep in my own bed tonight.

I walk down the sidewalk, making my way to the first driver. He has shaggy blond hair and piercing blue eyes—the kind that sees right through you.

I shiver and take a step back. "Uh, hey. Finally. We're so glad you're here. You have no idea."

"Yeah, sorry. Took a wrong turn," the guy says, exiting the truck.

Behind him, the other guy hops out of the second truck. He couldn't be more opposite to his partner, though. His bald head practically reflects the sunlight, it's so smooth, and his dark eyes are more suspicious than anything. Tattoos work up his forearms and I can't help but be a bit fascinated by the tribal markings. Despite their differences, they both wear the same uniform, if you can call it that. Jeans and a branded blue t-shirt with the moving company's logo embroidered on the left side.

"Well, you're here now," I say, shooting them a smile and hoping like hell it reaches my eyes. They'll be out of our hair soon enough. We may as well make nice. Otherwise, we'll find some of our stuff smashed up and favorite items missing, I have no doubt. I wave the two of them toward the house. "Let me show you around quick, that way you know which room is which."

They both nod, following behind me. By the time we enter the house, the two kids have vanished. Clearly, having returned to their lairs.

With both men at my back, I walk into the living room on the right. "So, obviously, this is the living room. Everything should be pretty well labeled. The couch, hutch, and bookshelf should all go in here," I say, pointing to their prospective locations.

As I turn around to face them, the blond guy steps forward abruptly, catching me off guard. He spins me around, planting a firm hand on my neck and squeezing tight.

CHAPTER 11
ENEMIES AND ALLIES
STONE

Alarm bells went off inside Stone's head the moment the moving truck pulled up. The hairs on the back of his neck rose and he fought the urge to shift here and now. The need to protect this woman and her children was rapidly growing stronger and he didn't know if it was because she was intriguing or if it was something far bigger. He hoped it was the former.

Yet, despite all of that, he worried more about what Ella would think if she knew he'd followed her back to her home. There was so much he didn't understand about what happened in that ravine, but it was nothing compared to the rude awakening barreling down on her. The last thing she needed was for him to blow her mind if it was all a false alarm.

However, anxiety curled through his midsection the moment she disappeared inside her house with the two men. While nothing seemed overtly unusual, he could just tell something wasn't right. He just couldn't put his finger on what exactly was triggering the concern.

Neither of them were Silas's men, he'd committed each of them to memory long ago, but he knew by now to trust his instincts.

The blond guy was way too eager to get inside and the bald one's lack of emotion concerned him nearly as much. Especially considering how late they were with the family's things. They should have been more apologetic and less...*whatever the fuck they were.*

No second thought needed, he dropped from his perch in the neighbor's large oak tree. He landed on her side of the fence without so much as a sound.

He quickly made his way to the moving van and opened the back gate.

Except for a few duffle bags, it was empty.

Even from the edge of her driveway, Stone heard Ella's squelched cry, and her heartbeat as it took off like a rocket. He was surprised at how fast he'd gotten used to the consistent thrum of her pulse, like a metronome keeping track of reality.

A muted thud followed her cry and all of Stone's plans went out the window, fleeing his brain like fog on a lake. He sprinted forward and leaped up the stairs three at a time, his heart suddenly hammering in his chest and keeping rhythm with hers.

Within seconds, he'd flung the door open, and

entered her living space. Despite only being in the home for a single night, her scent was everywhere. Under different circumstances, it would have been very distracting. But his senses were already heightened for battle.

He swung to the right and his eyes landed on the blond mover and his extended arm. His hand was wrapped around Ella's neck as he pinned her up against the wall. She was trying to pry the man's hands off but her efforts weren't very effective. However, relief and surprise flooded her features momentarily when she got sight of Stone.

It mixed with his relief and stirred up emotions better left pushed down for now.

On reflex, Stone shifted his gaze around the space. The bald one was nowhere to be seen. He was probably searching the house for the kids. Stone would deal with him next.

Confusion crossed the blond guy's features as he turned his blue eyes in Stone's direction. He clearly wasn't expecting interference with whatever the hell they had planned. While he didn't want to know, he had a suspicion, thanks to those bags in the back of the truck.

A growl erupted through Stone before he could stop himself.

The mover wasn't supernatural, but he was a threat all the same.

One Stone intended to eliminate.

"If you value that limb, drop it, and step away from her," Stone said, his words laced with malice. His animal tried to surface, wanting nothing more than to feast on the guy's entrails.

Funnily enough, the guy scoffed slightly, and his hand remained firmly grasped around Ella's throat. "And just who the hell are you? Their realtor?"

Stone didn't waste time mincing any more words. Instead, he stepped forward, sucker punching the guy in his exposed ribcage.

The blond guy's hand released on impact and Stone took advantage of it. He lunged forward, slammed his right hand across the man's throat, and drove him to the ground. Even without his supernatural strength, he could have taken this man down, but the added power, he was sure, got the message across that he was in charge now.

Ella scrambled away, coughing and sputtering as she took in more air. "Oh my god," she said. "Oh my god."

"Who sent you?" Stone asked. Another growl rode his words.

"What's it to—" the guy started.

Stone slammed his elbow across the man's nose. A fissure ripped across the blond's face and spewed blood across Ella's wooden floor.

"Silas something. That's all I know, man," the guy said, blinking away the tears that formed in his eyes from the blow. "We're just here to scare her."

Like hell.

At the sound of Silas's name and confirmation of his worst nightmare, Stone fought the urge to crush the man's windpipe.

Instead, his body went rigid as held back the need to shift and tear the guys beneath him limb from limb. He was almost certain his eyes had started to shimmer. "Leave this place. Run far, far away, and don't ever look back. If I see you anywhere near this family again, they'll never find your pieces. Do I make myself clear?"

It took every ounce of strength Stone had to loosen his grasp on the man and he was only doing it because Ella was gaping at them both.

"Found the kids—"

Stone's head snapped to the left to find the bald guy in the doorway with a kid's arm dangling from each fist. The teen boy was fighting back but didn't have enough strength to make a dent. The guy barely even blinked. The girl, on the other hand, was dead straight terrified. Stone could hear it in her heartbeat and see it on her face. She was frozen in fear, her eyes barely registering the scene in front of her.

"Avery, Asher—" Ella said, her voice rising an octave. She started forward, but the bald guy tilted his head in just a way that made her stop. Then he turned his gaze toward Stone and his partner.

Stone's hand slowly found its way back to the blond guy's upper torso, pinning him in place.

"Don't do anything stupid," Stone warned.

The bald guy chuckled and flitted his gaze between the two kids as if he was deciding which one to mess with first.

Ella let out a sob behind him and her desperation hit him in the gut like it was a physical thing.

Without hesitation, Stone lifted the guy beneath him off the floor a foot or so, then slammed him back down into the hardwood floor. The man lost consciousness instantly.

Humans are so easily damaged.

Stone was off him with the kind of speed only someone like him could tap into.

He hit the bald guy with so much force, he stumbled backward letting go of the girl completely but taking the boy down with him.

The girl squealed, as if coming back to life, and clawed her way to standing so she could run to her mom.

All three of them had hit the ground hard, each of them skidding across the floor in the momentum. The bald guy hit hardest and the impact knocked the wind entirely out of him. He dropped the kid and curled to the side, trying to get air into his lungs. But Stone was there to make that more difficult for him.

The boy scrambled away and raced back into the living room with his sister and mother.

Rage pumped through Stone's body and his animal begged him to be allowed to surface. Stone pushed him aside, as he worked out the best path forward. If he were to kill either of these men, Ella and her kids could be scarred because of it. And if Silas gets his way, and becomes Alpha, he'd likely retaliate in a big way.

No, he'd have to take care of these men discretely.

They'd have to disappear.

But even so... If Silas were to send any of the pack to the house, they'd know immediately Stone was involved. They'd smell him a mile away.

"Oh, thank God. Please, you have to send someone right away. Two men broke into my house and tried to hurt me and my kids. Please, send help," Ella said somewhere behind Stone. She rattled off the address and Stone realized this would work just as well, but he'd need to be long gone by the time the cops turned up.

He reared up, landing a decisive blow across the side of the bald guy's head.

Lights out.

Stone turned back to Ella. "Do you have any duct tape? Or some zip ties?"

Her jaw slacked open, terror still clear in her features. "Are you kidding me right now? I just moved in. I—I don't even have coffee in this damn house."

"Dammit," he sputtered, resting on his haunches and thinking.

The cops in town were good guys, but they could be easily swayed if Silas made his move. They want to keep their jobs, after all.

There was no way he was leaving Ella and her kids alone without the two men tied down—even if they weren't conscious. Instead, he would have to risk filing the cops in and hope like hell he could plead his case not to let it get back to Silas that he was here.

It was bad enough Silas killed his brother-in-law and got away with it...

Now he's after the one thing standing between him and becoming the next Alpha.

That means he knows Ella was bitten.

CHAPTER 12

IS NOTHING SACRED?

Clutching my cellphone in my hand like it's my only lifeline, I can't help but stare across the room in disbelief.

Someone just tried to kill me.

They tried to hurt my kids.

And they would have succeeded if...

My gaze flits to the mountain of muscle hovering over the bald guy.

Why is Stone here? *In my house?*

How on earth did he know we were in trouble?

My brain can't seem to latch onto anything sensible. It's like I've dropped into Wonderland and everything is topsy turvy.

And what about the way he moved? His speed and agility... It wasn't natural.

I shudder from the memory. It was intense and brutal, and, god help me, incredibly hot.

Or at least, it would have been if I wasn't about to piss myself.

Stone glances over his broad shoulder, his emerald gaze first landing on the blond guy knocked out the floor between us. After a moment, his discerning eyes flit to me. "Are you okay? Are you hurt?" His jaw quivers and he glances again at the man on the floor with a look that could kill. Still on his haunches, he doesn't make a move to stand.

I shake my head and rub at my throat. "Nothing I won't live from. Thanks to you."

My voice is raspy, but the throbbing has gone down some. Right now, I'm just incredibly happy to be alive and thankful my kids are okay. Scarred for life, maybe. But alive.

Stone nods and turns back to the bald guy beside him. I can't see Stone's face, but based on the moves he just pulled off, he must be mentally preparing for round two should the guy regain consciousness. If Stone didn't have some sort of military training, I'd be hella surprised.

"Stone...not that I'm not grateful, but what in the hell are you doing here?" I ask, unable to help myself.

The distant sound of sirens pulls my attention to the window and an ounce of relief floods through me. Soon, the assholes will be gone and this hellscape afternoon will be over.

"I..." he begins, his voice trailing off. A glint of surprise flits through his face

She knows my name?

The words tumble around in my head and catch me off guard. But not nearly as much as the strange rush of excitement riding behind them.

Before I can question it, Stone continues. "I was walking by when I heard someone scream. I didn't know it was your house."

Lies...

I narrow my gaze and tilt my head to the side.

"Mom," Avery squeals beside me. "The blond guy." She points, her finger shaking in the air as she does so.

My gaze extends to the man on the floor who nearly choked the life out of me. His eyelids flutter and his head lolls slightly to the right.

Something inside me snaps and I lunge forward, kicking him upside the head before I think better of it. Any signs of regaining consciousness are quashed instantly.

I glance up to surprise painted across Stone's face.

I shrug. "What? Hell if I was gonna let that asshat have a second try."

A grin tugs at his lips and he nods his head in approval. Then, he finally stands up and backs away from the door just as it swings open.

Three police officers, one woman, and two men enter. The woman has a slight build and strawberry blond hair pulled back into a tight, low bun. The men, on the other hand, couldn't be more different from each other. One is tall and lank and has a full head of curly brown hair. The other one is on the pudgy side, with less hair on his head than his face.

Each of them is wearing expressions of apprehension and alertness, as they should be. One by one, they take in the scene and then settle their attention on Stone. The four of them exchange a significant glance. They clearly know each other.

Stone raises his hands, but tips his head in the direction of the two movers. "These are the guys you're looking for."

Their attention swings from him to me.

The woman cop takes me in for a moment, her hazel eyes giving me the once over. "Ma'am? Are you the one who made the call?"

I nod, pointing to the floor. "Yes, these are the guys. Please, get them out of my house."

The bearded cop bends down, placing his fingers along the bald guy's neck. "This one's alive."

"Of course they're alive. We're not animals," I spit, my body beginning to convulse from the adrenaline still coursing through my body.

The woman cop steps over the bald guy's sprawled out legs and checks the blond's pulse as well. "Same. Let's get them to the station to sort this all out. Smith, call the EMTs and have them meet us there."

The lanky cop nods, grabbing a phone from his pocket. Then he steps out on the porch to make the call. The other two work to cuff the two men and prepare them for transport.

Stone eyes the cops in the house before saying, "Is it okay if I have a word with Officer Smith?"

The woman cop eyes her partner, but nods.

Without a second glance, Stone steps past the scene and out the door.

"Ma'am, we're going to need a full statement from you and the kids," the woman says.

I nod frantically. "Of course."

Avery clings onto my left arm, her small body trembling beside me. Asher stands just off to my right, barely moving a muscle—barely breathing.

I turn around to face them both. "Guys, I want you to both go in the kitchen and relax. Asher, call for a pizza or something. I know it's past lunchtime and we're all starving."

Asher nods but doesn't move a muscle.

"Go," I urge. The less they're around this mess, the better. Especially Avery. Her anxiety must be running rampant right now.

Avery reaches for Asher, clutching onto his arm and they both walk through the entryway, carefully stepping around the men. When they make it to the hallway that leads to the kitchen, their footsteps quicken.

They might fight like cats and dogs on a normal day, but at least when shit gets weird, they have each other's backs.

Suddenly, there's a flurry of activity as the bald guy starts to stir. The cop from outside barrels into the space, helping the bearded cop subdue him. Then two male cops drag baldy to his feet and escort him out of the house.

Some of the tension pooled in my center releases.

After a few seconds, Stone walks back in, his attention focused on the blond on the floor. The woman cop wears the same weary expression, as if waiting for the worst.

I, on the other hand, back up a bit, my right hand firmly clutched over my heart. When will all of this shit end?

Nothing about the start of this new chapter of our lives has gone the way I'd hoped.

"Do you think this was a crack house?" I blurt out.

I mean, why else would someone be trying to break in and snuff me and my kids out? Maybe there was something stashed on the property and we're in the way.

Stone snickers. "I highly doubt the St. Patrick's were running contraband from their house."

His handsome face is so damn smug and for a second, I just want to wipe that smirk off his face.

"How do you know?" I ask, jutting out my chin.

"They were both in their nineties," the woman cop responds, "and probably the sweetest old couple you'd ever meet."

My face flushes and I feel incredibly stupid for not knowing more about the previous owners. "Oh."

Well, there went that theory.

"Then...why the hell did these guys do this?" I ask, on the verge of tears. Goddamn, emotions anyway.

"We'll get to the bottom of that," the woman says, stepping up and out of the way when her male partners return. She's the one in charge—or at least, the one who doesn't have to do the grunt work.

The two men pick up the blond, hauling him out as well.

"All right, can you explain to me what happened?" she asks, pulling a small device out of her pocket. She clicks the side of it and holds it between the two of us.

"I thought they were my movers. Obviously, mine are running late," I say, opening my arms and suggesting to the open space of the living room. "But when we got in here, the blond guy..." I shudder, my memory flashing back to the sheer terror of being pinned to the wall with his hand around my throat.

I thought I was going to die.

Tears slide down my cheeks and I bite my lip to keep it from trembling. I swat at my tears, then run my fingertips across my forehead.

Suddenly, Stone is beside me, his warm hand pressing on the space between my shoulder blades. I glance up, appreciative and confused by his proximity.

Inhaling a jagged breath, I continue, "He, ah... didn't waste time. He surprised me, pinning me against the wall over there." I point to the spot beside our fireplace and shudder.

"He was strangling her," Stone finishes. "That's when I came in."

I nod. "He got the man to drop his hand and, well, you saw him."

"And how do the two of you know each other?" The woman asks, her eyebrow quirking up slightly as she shoots Stone a significant glance.

"We've bumped into each other around town, but I didn't know this was her place," Stone's dark eyes find mine and they hold a warning I'm not sure how to interpret. "I was out walking and heard her scream."

"So, you were just walking by and wanted to make sure she was okay?" the woman asks. For some reason, her BS meter must be going off. I can see it all over her face.

He shrugs. "Like I said, I had no idea who was in here. I just heard her scream and reacted."

"Uh-huh," she says, dropping her chin slightly. "And what about the other one?"

I bite my lower lip again. "He went looking for my kids. They were in their bedrooms and he—"

"They were here with violent intentions. The only thing in the back of their truck is a set of duffle bags," Stone says.

"And how do you know that?" the cop asks.

Stone winces slightly but presses his lips tight.

"Look, if it hadn't have been for Stone, we'd all be dead," I say with conviction.

She glances from me to Stone but doesn't say

anything else. However, I get the distinct impression more communication is going on than meets the eye.

"I'll need you to come down to the station for a full statement, Mr. Lachlan," she finally says.

He tips his head in acknowledgment.

She presses stop on the recorder and turns to me. "I'll also need you to come down, too, Mrs…"

"Ms.," I say, shuddering at the thought of being Mrs. anything. "Ms. Breene."

"We'll be in touch," the woman says, tipping her head.

"Shouldn't she have some additional protection?" Stone asks, his tone edgy and intense.

The woman quirks an eyebrow. "Do you have reason to believe this wasn't an isolated incident?"

He runs a hand along the back of his neck as a storm builds in his expression. "I'm not sure."

"Well then, we can increase patrols for the neighborhood, but that's about as far as I can go for the time being," she offers.

"Thank you. I appreciate that," I say, again fighting back tears.

Her lips press tight and her eyebrows tip up in the middle. "We need to document your attack, too. Would you prefer I send in some EMTs? Or would you rather head to the hospital?"

Panic races through me. Sending in people I don't know and trusting them at face value flashes me right back to the attack. But leaving the kids to go to the hospital is just as bad.

Realization slams into me and it's like being punched in the gut.

How in the hell am I ever going to feel safe alone in this house again?

Stone's hand returns to my back, somehow managing to ease my anxiety. "Send the EMTs. I'll stay with her to make sure she's okay."

CHAPTER 13
UNDER PRESSURE

ELLA

Nothing about this is okay.

Stone steps outside with the police and the second the extra people are gone, I collapse on the floor in the middle of my barren, god-forsaken living room.

I am not made for this kind of intense chaos.

"This was such a bad idea," I say, covering my face with my hands so my kids can't see my tears.

"Which part? Hiring a murderous moving company? Or moving in general?" Asher asks, plopping down next to me. His tone is flippant and I know he's doing what he always does... He's using his humor as a shield.

I glance up and shoot him a look of mild annoyance. A smile tugs at his lips, but he doesn't push it. Instead, he bends in close and rests his head on my shoulder. His presence calms my nerves and helps me relax a little. I close my eyes and lean my cheek against the top of his head.

Avery doesn't try to make light of things, like her brother. She takes up her spot on the other side of me, grabbing hold of my left arm and yanking it into her lap. I place my hand on her knee and give it a good squeeze.

These two are my life. I don't know what I'd do if anything bad had happened to them.

"Guys, I'm so sorry about all of this," I mutter. "I thought this would be the fresh start we were all looking for."

Neither of them moves or says anything at first and I glance down at Avery to get a better feel for her. She's the one I'm most worried about right now.

She glances up and nods. "Yeah, this has been ridiculously terrifying," Avery says, her voice barely a whisper.

"It's been a shitshow of epic proportions," Asher adds.

"Hey," I say, nudging him in the side with my elbow, "language."

But he's not wrong.

It *has* been a shitshow of epic proportions.

The front door opens and my heart jumps into my throat. But Stone walks back in, his green eyes surveying the scene until they land on me and the kids.

The storm that was brewing in his features releases. His eyebrows tip up in the middle and a smile plays at the corners of his lips when he sees the three of us.

"How's everyone doing in here?" he asks, walking into the space. His movements are so fluid and his style so put together, he feels out of place in this madhouse. He takes a seat, sitting cross-legged directly in front of us.

My eyes widen and I stare at the space between us. "Well, let's see... I should have known this day was going to be a disaster the moment I went to a coffee shop looking like a hot mess. After that humiliation, I ran into a grieving widow on my run, only to come home and nearly get murdered. So, I'd say...not my best day ever."

"Who is this guy?" Asher asks, leaning in.

I glance in his direction, realizing this is the first time the kids have met Stone.

Before I can open my mouth to explain, Stone extends his hand. "My name's Stone Lachlan. I'm—I guess I keep running into your Mom. I live in town."

Asher narrows his eyes.

Chuckling under my breath, I turn back to Stone and quirk an eyebrow. If he thought it was going to be easy to win over the hearts and minds of teenagers, he has sorrily misplaced his instincts.

Stone clears his throat and turns his gaze to me. "Did you say...you ran into my sister?"

"Technically," I lower my eyebrows, "no. I didn't say that."

His right eyebrow twitches, like he doesn't know whether to be impressed or annoyed at my attitude. "Okay, let me ask another way. Did you run into Clementine?" he asks directly, his eyes darkening.

I shrug, exhaling my reply, "Yes."

Avery turns to me, surprise written on her face. "You know this random dude's sister?"

"It's not like that. This is the guy I was telling you about yesterday. The one from the ravine. The one who,"—I glance between the two of them—"a-anyway, the man who died was his brother-in-law. He was the one who took on the wolves so I could escape."

Neither of them says anything at first and I have no idea why I feel so self-conscious about this. It's not like I asked Stone to come save our asses.

"You don't look like someone who could take on a pack of wolves. You look a little too..." Asher begins.

"Posh," Avery finishes.

Asher nods, extending his index finger like a gun and shooting it at her. "Yeah, that's it."

Stone's dark brows push into his hairline. "So, what does someone who can handle wolves look like?"

Asher shrugs. "I dunno, someone who wears overalls and has camo on."

Stone barks out a laugh. "Well, sorry to disappoint, but I have neither of those things in my wardrobe. But

I think I know a thing or two about wolves." He glances up at me, his eyes sparkling with the kind of intensity of someone who's got a secret they wish they could tell.

"I'm hungry," Asher says, leaning back on his hands. "How long do you think it will take for the pizza guy to get here?"

"And there you have it, folks. Teenagers and their gnat-like attention spans," I say, rolling my eyes to the ceiling.

Stone snickers softly.

"Thanks for saving my mom," Avery says. She's still latched on to my arm, but her voice is stronger than it was.

A full smile graces Stone's face and I can't help but admire the lightness of it. One thing's for sure, he's a damn handsome man and good in dire situations.

"It's the least I can do," he says, tipping his chin toward her. "What's your name?"

I run my hand over my face. "Oh my god, I'm so sorry. I should have introduced everyone."

Avery sticks out her hand. "Avery Hudson."

"Avery," he says, shaking her hand. "Nice to meet you."

She smiles, nodding her head as she takes her hand back.

Stone flits his gaze to Asher.

Ash chews on the side of his lip for a moment,

before extending his hand. "I'm Asher Hudson. My sister's right. Thanks for saving the day."

There's a hint of disappointment, or something like it, hidden in Asher's tone and I turn my questioning gaze to him. He ignores me, keeping his eyes planted on Stone.

Outside, a car door closes and I'm surprised when I catch the hint of pizza as the aroma wafts in.

"Your wish has been granted. Pizza's here," I say, turning to Asher.

"How do you—?"

A knock on the door makes both Avery and Asher jump. I start to get up, but Avery's grasp makes it almost impossible.

Stone catches my eye and it's as if a silent question is trying to push its way to me from those emerald eyes. But rather than voicing it, he stands up, holding a hand out. "Stay. I'll get it."

I settle back down, taking note of his confident swagger as he makes his way toward to door. While my nerves have calmed a bit, I'm still on edge and confused.

Plus, I still can't believe he's here. Of all the people to be wandering by when shit was hitting the fan...

Why him?

I'm so lost in my thoughts that it takes me a few seconds to realize Stone's not only getting the pizza from the delivery guy but he's pulling out his wallet, too.

"Oh, shit. Don't do that. Let me find my..." I glance around, completely discombobulated. "I have a purse here somewhere with some..." Even though the room is completely devoid of anything, I still look around like I should be tipping over couch cushions.

"You, too. Have a nice day," Stone says, handing the pizza guy cash and accepting an armful of pizza boxes.

There are far more boxes than necessary for the three of us. That's what happens when you leave a teenage boy in charge of ordering.

I hang my head, defeated.

Once the door is closed and the delivery guy has left, Stone turns to us and extends his arms. "Pizza?"

"Yes," Asher says, standing up like he's the Flash. He snatches the pizza boxes and makes a run for the kitchen with them.

"Manners," I call out after him.

His word echoes back from the empty kitchen, "Thanks."

Avery hangs fire, staying by my side as I get up and make my way to Stone.

"Do you want to have lunch with us?" I ask, tipping my head toward the kitchen. "I mean, you did pay for it and save our lives. I kinda feel it's the least we can do."

Stone laughs and the sound makes my insides flutter. His easy-going temperament and bold strength aren't like anything I'm used to. God knows the ex wasn't like that.

I could get used to having someone like him around.

Not that he's sticking around.

Oh god.

"Sure, I'd like that," he says, nodding.

For some stupid reason, my stupid heart trips over itself again. "Oh, good. That's awesome," I say, turning on my heel and feeling like a moron. I meander toward the kitchen with Avery and Stone in tow.

Asher has already demolished a few slices of pepperoni, but there are two other boxes of pizza to choose from. I point at the boxes spread across the counter. "Help yourself. I'd offer you a plate, but alas, my movers were homicidal lunatics."

"They weren't your movers," Stone says, reaching for a slice of triple meat pizza.

I take a slice of pizza covered in olives and tip my chin in his direction. "Yeah, I did pick up on that, actually."

Stone smiles and takes a bite. "So, what drew you to Black Crater?"

"We needed a fresh start," I say between bites.

"Ah," he responds as if it makes total sense without knowing the whole story. He turns to Avery. "So, you like TikTok?"

"How'd—?" Avery starts.

He raises a hand. "Educated guess. I work at the hospital and see a lot of teens roll through."

She settles back a bit and reaches for a cheese slice.

"She lives on TikTok," Asher says, wiping his mouth with the back of his hand.

Avery rolls her eyes. "At least I'm not obsessed with playing soccer *as a car.*"

"Rocket League is way more than—"

"Guys, no one cares," I say, splaying my hands out between them.

A smirk inches its way across Stone's face.

I inhale slowly and shake my head. "Sorry."

"No, it's all good. It's obvious you guys have a strong p—*family,*" he says.

"Yeah, now that Dad's a state away," Asher says, staring at his new slice of pizza.

I glance up into Stone's questioning eyes. "Didn't end well, huh?"

"That is a gross underrepresentation of events, but yes," I say.

"Hmmm," Stone mumbles, taking another bite.

"How about you? Are you—?" I say, unable to bring myself to say the "m" word.

He glances up, his piercing eyes burrowing through me. I hold my breath, waiting for his answer.

Finally, he shakes his head. "No."

"Oh," I whisper, taking another thoughtful bite.

Suddenly, my phone's ringtone goes off. I pat my

legs and realize I don't have my phone in these stupid sweats.

"Excuse me," I say, holding up a finger.

I follow the sound, walking back out into the living room.

My phone is on the floor next to the fireplace, a byproduct of the attack. I shudder, picking it up. The screen is cracked, making it almost impossible to see who's calling.

"Dammit," I mutter. Without thinking, I press the green answer button. "Hello?"

"Do you even know how to answer texts anymore? Or are you just trying to pretend I don't exist?" Troy says on the other end. "I have just as much of a right to talk to the kids as you do."

I roll my eyes and pinch the bridge of my nose. Why the hell did I answer it?

"Hello? Did you hear what I said?" Troy presses.

"I heard you."

"Then say something, goddammit. It's no wonder the kids don't know how to answer a damn phone call. Christ," he spits.

Fury unfurls inside me and I clench my fist, letting my fingernails did into my palms until it hurts.

"I assume that means the kids aren't answering you?" I say through gritted teeth.

"Nice observation. Maybe you can learn," he snickers.

"Fuck you, Troy."

He chuckles on the other end, clearly happy he got a rise out of me.

"Look, as much as I'd like to rehash the many failures of our lives together, I'm gonna have to pass. I've had a shit day and I'd like to keep it from getting any shittier," I say, glancing up to Asher, Avery, and Stone standing in the doorway, scrutinizing me.

I inhale sharply and walk out of their line of sight.

"Put Asher on the phone," Troy demands.

"No. We're eating lunch and we have company," I say.

"Who the hell would be visiting you?" he asks indignantly.

"That's none of your goddamn business."

"I should be able to know who's around my—"

Anger boils through my veins and I can hardly stop myself from seeing red. "No. You're not talking to them and we're *not* doing this. *Fuck off.*" A surge of energy rolls through me and I hang up the phone before he can make any further comments.

I clutch the phone in my hand, visualizing strangling Troy as my fist tightens.

With a deep breath, I shake it off, and walk back to the kitchen.

The three of them are crowded around the island, pretending they hadn't heard the whole exchange just now.

Holy shit, I'm glad it's not me she's pissed at.

"Oh, shut it, Asher," I spit. "Now's not the time."

Stone's eyes widen and he glances between me and my son.

"I didn't say anything," Asher says. His brown eyes are wide and the color drains from his face.

"What are you talking about? I heard you..." I look around the room, eyeing each confused face.

"He didn't say anything, Mom," Avery says, shaking her head. "Are you okay?"

CHAPTER 14
LAW OF THE BITTEN
STONE

I f there were any doubts before, there were none left after witnessing Ella on that call.

Stone smiled to himself.

Doug pulled off what Stone never thought he'd have the balls to do. He blocked Silas from becoming Alpha.

They'd both known Silas had plans in motion to shift allegiances, but Doug had doubted his Beta would go as far as murder to get what he wanted. That doubt cost him his life.

Now, against all odds, Ella Breene is destined to become the next Alpha of the Black Crater Pack. And she's hopelessly clueless.

If she could stay alive long enough to shift for the first time, she might have a chance. But the odds aren't in her favor. Silas has already tried to cut his potential loose ends, even without proof she was a threat.

The extent to which Silas has been willing to go is astounding, but Stone shouldn't be surprised. Silas was the reason the pack had shunned Stone in the first place. But if he had tried to warn the pack, after everything, it would just come off like petty vindictiveness.

Stone didn't have time for that bullshit.

Yet, somehow, without even realizing it, without knowing it was a possibility even... Ella had tapped into her Alpha voice.

The power that rolled through her command was enough to make Stone snap to attention.

As the pack's Omega, that's saying something.

In some ways, that suited him fine. It made him harder to control. Not that it was an easy feat, to begin with.

Yet, somehow, he was compelled to obey, just the same.

Hell, the command wasn't even for him.

He could only imagine what the guy on the other end of the line must have thought.

Then again, mundane humans could be absurdly oblivious. By the sound of things, that one more than most.

Regardless, if Stone was going to be able to protect Ella and her kids—and keep Silas from taking over as de facto Alpha—it would mean having to invoke the *Law of the Bitten.*

Doing something like that without absolute proof

won't go down without a challenge. But it could be the only hope Ella has to stay alive.

He needed to summon a pack meeting before Silas tried again to end his competition.

"Thank you so much for dinner," Stone said, as he edged near the door. "You know, I should really be going."

Ella's eyebrows rose into her hairline. "I thought you were going to stay until the EMTs arrived."

She didn't say it out loud, but it was clear to him that being left alone right now was freaking her out. Even if she didn't know him, she trusted him enough to keep her safe. Unexpected warmth spread through his torso.

Stone brushed his fingertips across his lips. "No, yeah... You're right. Sorry, I was getting ahead of myself. I didn't want to impose, but I can stay. "

He'd forgotten about the EMTs. The markings on her neck had already vanished and he knew better than most how fast a werewolf heals as they closed in on their first shift. They wouldn't find anything wrong with her.

Just then, Stone heard the slamming of a vehicle's doors.

Seth's muffled thoughts tumbled at him like a gnat buzzing around his head.

Thanks to his Omega status, he couldn't quite make out his pack mate's thoughts as clearly as he could when he was a full member of the pack.

However, he could still sense the energy of their owner.

Good timing.

Stone's anxiety lessened a bit. Seth was loyal to Doug and he'd take good care of Ella and the kids. Whoever was with him as his partner today wasn't a part of the pack.

Ella turned toward the doorway at the same time Stone did. Her increased sense of hearing was already kicking in.

"Someone's here," she announced, as a hint of panic flashed across her beautiful face.

For as long as he could remember, he'd been a loner. Someone who would rather spend his time trying to find a cure to the madness that had infected them both, rather than find a mate. But lately, he found himself wishing he could keep that fear on her face at bay. The desire to protect her was growing and he didn't understand why.

Was it always this way with a new Alpha?

He held out a hand. "Stay here. I'll see who it is."

Fear shone in the faces of the two kids, but without waiting for their responses, Stone left the kitchen and made his way to the front door.

He could only imagine how this change would tip their world upside down when it actualized.

While he couldn't hear Seth's complete thoughts, Stone knew his scent. He could also smell the medical bag Seth or his partner carried on the other side of the door. The objects inside carried a distinctive odor he'd gotten very accustomed to at the hospital.

"Hey, Seth. Gordon," Stone said, tipping his head at each of them as he opened the door.

Seth's dark eyes flashed with curiosity, but he knew better than to say anything out loud.

Gordon's blue eyes widened with surprise. His red hair stood on end like he'd just gotten out of bed. His freckles were blotchy, likely a result of a hard night of partying.

"What are you—?" Gordon began.

Seth placed a hand on his partner's shoulder. His dark skin was in deep contrast to the white of his partner's EMT uniform. "Duty first." Seth then turned to me. "Stone, where are the woman and her two kids?"

Stone stepped aside and pointed to the kitchen. "Back there."

The two of them nodded and continued past him.

For a moment, he stuck his head out the door and perked his ears. No one else from the pack was nearby and as far as he could tell, everything was as it should be.

That was a good sign.

Things should be on the up and up.

If he could get Seth on his side, Stone might have a chance toward winning the pack over with his invocation. If nothing else, maybe he could get Seth to stay behind and protect Ella and her family until he could return. Either would be ideal.

Stone turned on his heel and followed after the paramedics. By the time he entered the kitchen, Gordon and Seth were already hard at work. Seth was inspecting Ella's neck, while Gordon was giving the daughter a once-over.

Stone stood back, leaned against the wall, and observed the room. As an immunologist, he had more medical training than the two of the EMTs combined. But it was best, he'd found, to let people do their jobs without interference.

Sure, he could have tried to warn Seth through their pack bond, but it was doubtful he'd be able to pick up on all of Stone's thoughts anyway. And it could mean alerting others in the pack to what was up. Instead, he would talk to Seth the old-fashioned way.

Besides, when it came to Ella, he already knew they wouldn't find anything wrong with her.

Thanks to her imminent shift, Ella would be in perfect health. Better than she was a couple of days ago, he wagered. The kids, on the other hand, he hadn't really assessed, but based on his limited observations, they were scared, not hurt.

After the longest twenty minutes of his life, the assessment was finally over as Seth declared, "You'll be okay. Your trachea is fine and there's no lasting damage that I can see."

Then, he turned and shot Stone a significant glance. A question appeared in his eyes.

Stone took that as his cue. "Seth, can I have a word?"

Gordon and Seth glanced at each other.

Seth nodded. "Sure."

Stone walked out of the room and made his way for the front porch. He needed a bit of privacy for what he was about to say.

Once the door was closed behind them, he inhaled slowly and released the breath. "Seth, we have a problem."

"I kinda figured. What's going on?"

"That woman in there..." he began, unsure of the direction he should take. He finally spat out, "She was bitten by Doug."

Seth blinked a few times without saying anything.

"I'm sure Silas has already tried to claim—" Stone continued.

Seth raised a hand. "Yeah, that asshat already laid claim, but if Doug chose someone else, that changes everything."

Stone nodded in agreement. "Ella was attacked because Silas knows."

Seth's eyebrows tighten. "Are you sure?"

Stone pressed his lips tight and nodded.

"Then you have to invoke the—"

"I know. But I need to make sure Ella and the kids are safe while I'm gone. Silas killed Doug, I won't allow him to kill..." his words petered out. He hadn't told anyone about Doug. And he sure as hell didn't want to consider Ella being murdered.

"That's a serious accusation," Seth said, his voice a hushed whisper.

"It's not an accusation. I watched it happen." Stone flashed a warning with his eyes.

Seth leaned in. "Holy shit. Why didn't you bring this to the council?"

"Because I've been a little preoccupied keeping that woman in there safe," he said and jabbed a finger toward the house. "She's a walking nightmare without a clue what's going on."

"You haven't told her?" Seth asked.

"No, I—" Stone shook his head. "I haven't had a great opportunity. What with the attack and all. And to be fair, I wasn't positive she was turning until a few minutes ago. I didn't see Doug bite her—but I felt it. Or something when I stumbled on the two of them. But today, I witnessed her tapping into her power. I have no more doubts."

"That explains the lack of evidence from her attack. I mean, there's literally *no sign* whatsoever." Seth heaved out a breath. "Go, I'll hold down the fort here. The pack is already divided since Doug's death."

"Murder," Stone corrected.

Seth nodded, then shuddered. "Murder. If Silas gets his way, the pack is going to self-destruct."

Stone heaved a sigh. "If they don't accept the invocation, it already has."

CHAPTER 15

WHAT'S HAPPENING TO ME?

ELLA

The redheaded paramedic leans against the island, tapping his fingertips against the edge. "So, just moved here, eh?"

I shoot him a faux-befuddled glance. "No, why do you ask?"

He stands up straighter, confusion waring in his features. "I mean... Well, I thought..."

"Mom," Avery groans.

"I'm just messing with you," I say, swiping my hand through the air. "It's been a long day and I deflect through inappropriate and ill-timed humor."

He chuckles under his breath. "Oh, well, good one."

I raise my eyebrows and snicker—more at myself than him. "We just moved in yesterday, but our stuff hasn't arrived yet."

"We thought the guys who attacked us were the

movers. So..." Asher says, frowning. "Can we not talk about this? It's kind of a touchy subject at the moment."

Red sucks air through his teeth and cringes. "Oooh, harsh. Sorry, man. That musta sucked."

"You could say that," I mutter under my breath.

"They got the bad guys, though. Right?" he asks, turning to look down the hallway.

The front door opens and relief warms my center. As nice as the redhead paramedic is, trusting anyone new right now is pretty much not gonna happen. The only one who's proven himself is Stone, even if I still don't understand how all of this happened. I'm equal parts grateful and irritated that it was him who saved the day.

I suck in a breath as he enters the room. There's something about the way he moves that sets me on fire in a way I have no business being lit. Half of me craves the feelings he evokes. But the scared, sane half thinks I'm as nuts as I feel and I need to carry on with my spinster future without trying to dive headlong into some sort of romantic crush.

Stone makes his way over, stopping when he's directly in front of me. "Ella, I wish I could stay longer, but I really need to be going," he says, his eyebrows tugged in tight.

A wave of disappointment washes over me and I fight back the sudden dread the prospect of being left alone unleashes. As much as I don't need a man in my life, God knows I don't... I also wasn't expecting to be attacked in my own home. It sure felt good knowing Stone was here. Both during and after the attack. I don't think I would have been able to turn the tables on my own and that feeling of helplessness is terrifying. We could all be dead right now if it wasn't for him.

But, yeah, I get it.

It's not like we're a couple, so of course, the guy's gotta get on with his life.

"Oh, right," I mutter. Despite the myriad of things I'd like to say, it's the only thing that escapes my lips.

As if reading my disappointment, something that would have been unheard of with the ex, he steps forward and places his hands on my upper arms. "Don't worry. I'll be back to check on you all. I just have some things I need to attend to. But Seth has agreed to stay here until I get back." Stone turns to the dark-skinned paramedic and places a hand on his shoulder. "Seth is a friend. And you shouldn't be alone right now."

Hopefully, Silas won't try again so soon.

"Who's Silas?" I ask before I can stop myself. I blink quickly, stepping out of Stone's hold. "I'm sorry, I don't know why I said that."

Stone's face goes ashen and the whites of his eyes have taken up more space. He tilts his head slightly to the side and shoots a glance at the paramedic. "Uh, I'll be back as soon as I can. Try not to get into any more trouble."

I stick out my chin. "No promises."

A slight smirk plays at the edges of his lips and he nods. Then, without another word, he walks out of the kitchen, making his way to the front door before vanishing before my eyes.

I let out a deep sigh. When I turn back to the room, everyone is staring at me.

"What?" I shrug.

"Could you pine a little less obvious? It's grossing me out," Avery says, making a face.

"I wasn't. I was—" I glance at the two paramedics, who have suddenly found the floor very fascinating to look at. "Anyway..."

"I should be going, too," Red says, barely meeting my gaze. "I need to get the ambulance back."

I glance over at Seth. "Are you sure you can stay? I mean, I don't want to keep you from something important. Shouldn't you be saving more lives?" I point toward Red.

Seth shakes his head. "My shift ended a half-hour ago. You were my last stop of the day anyway. It's no big deal. Gordon can handle the rest."

Red, aka Gordon, nods, but for a split second, the expression he has says he's confused.

I place my hands on my hips and bust out my *Mom voice*. "Gentleman, if you're lying to me, so help me..."

Seth winces slightly.

I narrow my gaze and wait.

Shit, shit...

After a few seconds, he squirms under my scrutiny. "Look, I promised Stone I'd stay. It's no big deal."

I shake my head. "No way. I will not be the reason you get fired." I plant my hands on Seth's shoulders and spin him toward the door.

"Really, it's not a problem," Seth protests.

"Mom, if he wants to stay, shouldn't we—" Avery snaps her mouth shut when she sees my expression.

"Look, I appreciate your support, and trust me, it means a lot that you're willing to stay. But I just can't justify it. The cops are going to increase patrols. I'm sure we'll be fine." Even as I say it, my insides coil. I don't want to be left alone, and the fact that Stone vouches for him does make me feel better. But I refuse to accept help when it could put this guy's job in jeopardy.

She'll make a good Alpha.

"What did you say?" I ask, lowering my eyebrows. Alpha?

Seth's eyes widen. "I didn't say anything."

I clench my jaw. I know what I heard, but I just don't understand what it means. "Fine, whatever. It was nice to meet you both. I appreciate your help, but I got it from here." In what should have been a cool movement, I step out in front of the two of them but misjudge the doorframe. My left shoulder slams into it and I grope at my upper arm. "Mother trucker."

Reflexes haven't kicked in yet.

I spin around. "What?"

Everyone behind me shakes their head.

I run my fingertips over my right eyebrow. What in the actual?

Inhaling sharply, I spin around and march toward the front door. When I get there, I yank it open and wait for the EMTs to follow.

As Seth reaches me, he stops and says, "It's no trouble. Stone seemed really—"

I smile, but I know it doesn't reach my eyes. "Thank you both." I flit my gaze to Gordon and back to Seth.

Thankfully, he gets the hint and bows his head before walking out.

When they've both exited the house, I close the door and flip the deadbolt into place. Closing my eyes, I lean my back against the door, letting my head fall back to the wood.

What a day...and it's only early afternoon.

Asher walks up. His eyes carry the same weariness I feel. Without saying a word, he reaches out, wrapping his gangly arms around me. Before I know it, Avery is in the mix, doing the same. I tug them in close as tears stream down my cheeks.

If I had lost them...

I clutch them both closer. "I'm so sorry, guys."

"It's not your fault," Asher says softly.

"Yeah, except I moved you here. I let the homicidal guys into the house..." I start.

"How were you to know they weren't the movers? I

mean, that was pretty darn coincidental," Avery says. "How did they know we're waiting for our stuff?"

I shake my head, still holding them both in tight. "I have no idea."

"That guy who saved us—" Asher starts.

"Stone," I say.

"He knows more than he's letting on," Ash continues.

"What do you mean?" I ask.

He steps out, his jaw hardening. "He asked who sent them—like he knew they were working for someone else."

"He did, didn't he..." I say, thinking.

"Yeah, and the guy said 'Silas something.' Then you said his name back in the kitchen. What's going on?" Avery asks. Her brown eyes plead with me to make sense of all the insanity.

"I honestly have no idea..." I whisper.

"Mom, ever since we got here...it's like something's off with you. Do you think you got tetanus from that guy in the ravine?" Asher asks, his expression darkening.

While anything is possible, I don't feel like that's it. If anything, I feel better than ever.

"No, I don't think so, honey. I think I'm just jumpy after everything that's happened. We just need things to get back to normal."

Suddenly, my phone rings, making all three of us jump.

I clutch at my heart but reach for my phone. From what I can make through the cracks, I think the number is for the moving company. Inhaling sharply through my nose, I answer. "Hello?"

"Ms. Breene?" a woman's voice on the other end responds.

"Yes."

"This is Ms. Green from Tabula Rasa Movers," she announces. "I just wanted to call to inform you that the movers are on their way to you. They ran into some car trouble when they entered Oregon, but they should be there within the next half hour."

My heart leaps into my throat. "Great. We won't be at the house, though. Tell them there's a key under the front doormat."

"Will do. So sorry for the trouble."

"Thanks for the update," I say, then hang up the phone. I turn to both of the kids. "Get your things. We're leaving the house for a bit."

They both stare at me with questioning gazes.

"The movers are almost here," I say.

"On it," Asher says, not sticking around a moment longer.

"Wait for me," Avery calls out, chasing after him.

After everything that's gone on, the last thing I'm going to do is be here when those movers arrive. We were never meant to be here, as it was. They can handle bringing things in without us now.

I make my way from the front entry to the kitchen,

trying to remember where I put the keys to the High-lander. I find them on the counter in the kitchen, next to my purse. Collecting both, I make my way back to the entry.

The sooner we're outta here, the better.

"Stone, we have a problem. She's kicked us out," Seth says.

I glance around, startled. His voice sounds like he's standing right beside me, but he's gotta still be outside. And if that's the case, there's a whole house between us.

Crazier yet, I hear Stone's side of the conversation. "Dammit. Okay, stay nearby and keep an eye on her that way. I've just summoned the pack. I should be able to start the invocation soon."

"Got it," Seth says. "Hurry. She's gonna need answers soon."

"I know."

The conversation ends and silence fills the emptiness left behind.

I walk over to the decorative window to the right of the front door. Sure enough, Seth is standing in the middle of my yard. He doesn't get into the ambulance with Gordon, either. He continues past it and hits the sidewalk before he vanishes beyond our fence.

Gordon starts up the ambulance and backs out of my driveway all alone.

Exhaling the breath I was holding, I stare absently at the end of the driveway.

There's no way I should have been able to hear that conversation. Thanks to years of loud concerts, my hearing isn't what it used to be. So, how the hell did I make out every word?

More importantly, what the hell is going on?

No, scratch that.

What the fuck is happening to me?

CHAPTER 16
INVOCATION
STONE

Leaving Ella and her kids with Seth felt like the right thing to do at the time, but the further Stone got from her presence, the more uncomfortable he felt. For some bizarre reason, it was like a piece of him had strayed too far from its home and he needed it returned.

It was agitating, considering he could travel as far from his pack as he'd wanted before.

So, what was this all about?

Maybe it was because she kicked Seth out of the house, so he had to keep guard from a different vantage point.

Whatever it was, he'd have to worry about it later. Right now, he had to figure out how to protect Ella from any more of Silas's attacks.

Silas was operating under the assumption no one

knew about Ella, but that illusion was about to come crashing down.

Once Stone reached the woods, he stripped off his clothes and shifted into his wolf form. He could reach the Sacred Grove faster that way and chances were, everyone else would arrive in wolf form, anyway. They were less vulnerable and they'd be suspicious as fuck since he was the one to call the meeting.

Besides, Stone knew all too well that if he were to have any chance of getting a word in edge-wise, he'd need to be there before the majority of the pack arrived. If he didn't initiate the conversation, Silas would dominate the narrative and that would be the end of that.

After all, what place did Stone have to disrupt the Alpha selection process?

He was barely even considered one of them.

Silas had already seen to that.

Fucking asshat.

One way or another, Stone was determined to be the thorn in Silas's side that just wouldn't go away. He'd fester there until Silas crawled back into the hole he came from. Silas might think he'd gotten away with killing the pack's Alpha without repercussions, but he was about to learn the hard way that wasn't the case.

Stone wasn't sure what kind of Alpha Ella would be, but he had zero doubts she'd be better than Silas.

But first, she needed a damn chance.

He padded his way into the moss-covered stone

circle in the middle of the woods. Thankfully, as he approached, Stone breathed a sigh of relief. He was the second one there—arriving only after his sister.

As expected, she too, was in her wolf form. That meant the rest would arrive the same.

While the two of them were from the same family and were born into this curse, Stone was the only pure white wolf he knew. The rarity of it had always made his sister jealous and others hate him.

However, Clementine's gray and white marbled fur fit in better with the others in the Black Crater Pack. The majority of them were adorned with dark or marbled fur. However, the white she did have still made her stand out enough that she had drawn the attention of the Alpha.

Doug and Clem's love story had always made Stone jealous, even if he'd never admit that to a single soul. Not even her. Though he had been ridiculously happy for her.

He just wished he'd find someone who made him as happy as Doug had made her.

Yet here she was now, with no time to grieve her dead husband—her mate. Instead, she was just as determined as Stone was to ensure the pack was left in good hands. She knew better than most how dangerous Silas could be.

She also knew Doug's death was no accident as much as he did.

Are you ready for this? Her thoughts tumbled at Stone as she stood up, shaking off her anticipation.

Because of their blood connection, he could hear her in his mind just fine. She would be the only one, though. The moment the rest of the pack arrived, the voices would dim or garble together, and he'd be at a severe disadvantage.

All thanks to the semi-banishment.

As ready as I'll ever be. He responded.

She nodded and walked in a semi-circle around him. *He won't accept this claim without a fight.*

I know. But there are no other options. Doug made his choice. Ella deserves a chance. Stone said.

She nodded her agreement.

The familiar static of the other pack members arriving began to cause Stone's connection to falter. He hoped he'd be able to relay his message without having to shift back into human form. But he would if all else failed. This was too important to let it get lost in translation.

Within minutes, more than thirty members of the Black Crater Pack were convened at the Sacred Grove. It was more than he expected, but there were still plenty of them who didn't bother turning up or taking his plea seriously.

Oddly enough, Silas was the last to arrive.

He slunk into the midst of the other wolves, his dark fur an ominous sign for the type of leader he'd be if his claim were left unchecked. Silas's deep brown eyes were nearly red as they flit from wolf to wolf. *What is the meaning of this?* He asked. His words carried the weight of an Alpha but lacked their full power.

Stone would know—he'd felt the intensity of Ella's command.

This was more like a child pretending to be a parent.

Stone pawed his way into the middle of the circle. It was now or never.

All eyes were on him, and he fought to drown out the confused static.

I'm here to invoke the Law of the Bitten, he said, amplifying his declaration and hoping it came through clearly. He knew he had to get straight to the point before his intentions were drowned out.

What?

What did he say?

Bitten?

How is this possible?

He can't be serious.

The thoughts of the others were jumbled together but he got the gist. They were as surprised as he expected them to be. Silas had likely been making it seem as though he was their only option.

Stone circled the pack, staring each one in the eye before he said, *Doug chose his successor and it wasn't Silas.*

A couple of pack members growled in response. Likely Silas's lackeys.

Then who? Stone turned toward the thought, which surprisingly came through loud a clear. He walked over to Marta. Her golden eyes were locked on his, but curiosity played at their edges.

Don't be ridiculous. Doug died in a freak accident. There was no one around when it happened. Stepping into the center of the circle with Stone, Silas's words were hard to make out.

However, Stone expected no less than a full-on denial from him. He was also smart enough to know that calling him out on Doug's murder would be a death sentence for not only himself but Ella and her kids.

This was still the safest bet.

Stone squared up to Silas. He had a good few inches on Silas, but he knew he didn't have the same support from the pack. *Then why did you send people to kill her?* Stone asked.

Silas snorted and continued to circle Stone. *That's absurd.*

Doug bit a woman? Marta asked. Excitement tickled at the edge of her mental tone and Stone hoped he could play on that. Marta was a badass, for sure, and she always wanted the females of the pack to have more say. With Ella in charge, that was certainly a possibility.

Stone turned toward her. *Yes. He bit a woman.*

That's— she began.

Enough. I can't believe any of you are even playing

into this. This is Stone, we're talking about. If anything, this is nothing more than a desperate outcast grasping at straws so he can be relevant again. Silas snarled. *Doug would never have bitten a woman. He never would have bitten* anyone.

And yet, he did. Clementine said, stepping up beside Stone. She raised her snout high, eyeing each one of the pack members.

Pride flooded through Stone and for the first time in a long time, he felt supported—*validated.*

Of course, you'd take his side. Silas spat, shaking his head. *You couldn't just be by my side, the way you had been with Doug. I would have welcomed you as one of my mates. But no, you'd rather choose exile with your brother?*

You are not our Alpha. Not until the full moon has risen and the pack has chosen. Clementine declared. *Doug chose his successor and we must respect that choice. I've seen her with my own eyes and felt her power rising. I can't explain why he did it or when it happened, but it did. When the rest of the pack realizes it, they'll bow to her. I second Stone's motion to invoke the Law of the Bitten.*

A low rumble rolled through Silas. Several other wolves followed suit, growling their disapproval with Clementine's declaration.

Stone noted every one of them. They were nearly split down the middle. If things went sideways, and they likely would, they would be in for a hell of a fight.

He hoped it wouldn't come to that.

For now, Clementine's proclamation was strong.

The pack would comply, even if they weren't going to agree with Stone.

Silas stopped moving, his red eyes speaking of malice and death as they landed on Stone and his sister. *If you think this* human *was bitten,* Silas began. Disdain dripped from his tone, even in mental form, *bring her to us tonight. I formally challenge her claim.*

CHAPTER 17
WHAT IN THE ACTUAL?

ELLA

"Where are we gonna go?" Avery asks, clicking her seatbelt into place.

Asher assumes his position in the front passenger seat and shoots me the same expectant gaze.

I shrug slightly before putting the Highlander into reverse. "I don't know. All I do know is that I'm going to be as far away from the house as possible when those movers turn up."

"Agreed," Asher says, inhaling loudly through his nose.

"Can we hang out at the mall?" Avery asks.

I glance at her through the rearview mirror. "Sweetie, this town is pretty small. I'm not entirely sure they *have* a mall."

"You moved us to a town with no mall?" Her mouth gapes open, unleashing her angsty teen vibes.

I chuckle under my breath. "I mean, I don't know for sure..."

"Why don't we just go to a movie or something? That'll occupy a couple of hours and I won't wish for the good old times when I was being held hostage," Asher says, shooting me a look. "Then we can grab supper and hopefully come home to a house full of clutter and no homicidal movers."

My eyebrows rise. "It's weird when you sound like the reasonable one."

"Well, someone has to be," he claps back.

"Oooh, well played." I chuckle. "Sorry, Avery, but I think Asher has won this one."

Avery crosses her arms over her chest. "That's fine. I wanted to see the new Ghostbusters movie anyway."

"Yeah, me too," Asher says, nodding.

"Well, that settles that," I say, driving toward town and hoping it's the right direction. "Find the nearest theater and showtimes."

Nearly five hours and two calls from the movers later, we're on the way back from our town-bound excursion.

The movie was decent, though it certainly could have been better. The sushi, on the other hand, had been great. And overall, the time out together had been exactly what we needed. In an effort to rewrite the day, I even took the kids for ice cream.

The last few hours were the most normal part of the move to Oregon so far.

I can only hope there'll be many more times like it.

However, the drive home puts me on edge. I don't know if it's the anxiety of returning to the house or the fact that we'd have to return to reality. Then, there are moments where I swear I can sense Stone nearby—which is utterly ridiculous.

Way more often than I'd care to admit, my mind rolls back to those moments before we left when I swear I could hear conversations I should never have been able to hear. Like the one with Seth talking on the phone to Stone...

It was like they were talking gibberish. They threw around words like invocation and pack...but they were all out of context and if I'm totally honest, they kinda scared the shit out of me.

"Mom, look out—" Asher says, bracing his hands on the dashboard.

I blink away my thoughts and slam on the brakes as a pure white wolf runs out in front of us. It settles itself on the ridge on the other side of the road, watching us like I'm the dumbass.

"Goddammit, what's with the wolves in this area?" I spit, cramming my heart back into my chest. "Do they have a death wish?"

"I think it's the same one from before," Avery says.

"I'm sure there are lots of white wolves, sweetie. There's no way it's the same—"

"But I remember those eyes," she says. Her gaze is locked on the wolf when I check on her in the rearview mirror.

By the time I turn back, it's vanished into the treeline.

"All I can say is we better not witness another car accident," Asher mutters, keeping his eyes fixed on the road in front of us.

The evening sun is setting behind the trees, but it's not quite dark yet. It's the magical space between day and night.

"That makes two of us," I blurt out, putting my foot back on the accelerator, driving slower than I had been before.

"There's another one," Avery says, pointing to her window.

I look over my shoulder and sure enough, a white and gray wolf has taken to running the ridge on our left. There's something about it that almost stops me in my tracks.

There's something so familiar about them both...

"Where'd the other one go?" I ask, suddenly weary. I slow the vehicle down some more and scan the space as diligently as possible. The last thing I'd want to do is hit the white wolf because of my inattention.

"I don't know. I don't see it," Avery says, peering through the window.

"We're almost home. I'm surprised they're willing to get this close to a residential area," I mutter under my breath. I hope like hell they head back the way they came before we get to our house, but I'm not so sure that's their agenda.

She's nearly there.

The thought intrudes my mind and I glance over at the wolf. It continues to run alongside our vehicle, keeping pace like it's no big deal to run forty-five miles an hour.

However, when I click on the blinker to turn right, the white and gray wolf slows, then takes a seat at the small hill that ends with the intersection.

I exhale my relief. "It's not following us anymore."

A few minutes later, I pull into my driveway.

Sitting on the porch steps is Stone. With his head down and hands in-between his knees, his silhouette is pronounced in the light of the porch. He's clad, once again, in beach shorts and nothing else.

I can't tear my eyes away from his broad shoulders and defined chest muscles.

"What's he doing here?" Asher asks, voicing the first thing that came to my mind as well.

"He's probably checking to make sure we're okay. He seemed pretty adamant about protecting us," I say, my words petering out as I see the look on Stone's face.

I put the Highlander in park and exit immediately. "What is it? What's wrong?"

Stone glances up and the anguish pulsing through his aura amplifies. His dark eyebrows tug in, but no words escape.

"Ah, Christ," I mutter, fumbling for my keys.

Avery and Asher exit the vehicle behind me, slowly making their way forward.

"Well, come in. I'm sure whatever's got your knickers in such a twist is going to require alcohol," I say, sliding the key in the lock. "I can't promise I'll be able to find any since I wasn't here when the actual movers dropped off our shit, but I'll see what I can do."

When the lock clicks back and I move to open the door, I half expect to find the house exactly the way I left it. To my glorious surprise, there's a couch in my living room and boxes stacked neatly against the wall. I catch a glimpse of my dining table on the other side and there is evidence the movers have been very careful about matching up the labels with their respective rooms.

They must have felt guilty as fuck for being late.

Point scored for the Breene house. About goddamn time, too.

"Yessss—" Asher says, racing to the living room and dive-bombing the couch. He rolls around on it like it's his long-lost friend. "I've missed you so much."

I roll my eyes and turn back to Stone. "So, what is it I can do for you now?"

Avery slinks up the stairs, likely excited to get

moving on decorating and rearranging her new room. Chances are, I won't see her for days now.

Stone's green eyes darken and he flicks them over to Asher quickly before locking in on me. "Can we speak somewhere private?"

"Oh, hell-to-the-no, buddy. I've had enough with crazy dudes for one day. Anything you gotta say to me can be said open and in public of my domicile. I hide nothing from these kids," I say, holding my chin up.

"What's a domicile?" Asher asks, his head bobbing up like whack-a-mole from the other side of the couch's arm.

Stone snickers softly. "Share everything except your vocabulary, it seems."

I slap him on the chest with the back of my hand and instantly regret it. A pang of something that feels suspiciously like lust crawls across my skin and slithers southbound.

I wish he'd put a shirt on.

"Seriously, what do you need? I have a bedroom to rearrange here, too," I say, clamping my mouth shut.

Why the bedroom? Why did I have to say the bedroom? I have a whole house to unpack.

I run my hand over my face.

"I don't think you're going to like what I have to say," Stone says, the veins on the side of his jaw popping out as he clenches it tight.

"Wow, okay, Mr. Cryptic. Can you be any more vague?" I say, meandering toward the kitchen.

This is definitely going to require a drink.

He follows behind me, not saying a word. Instead, a thought keeps playing over and over in my mind.

She'll never believe me.

Thankfully, there's a box on the kitchen counter labeled glasses. I rip open the tape and pluck two of them from its innards. Spinning on my heel, I assess the other boxes quickly and locate the Holy Grail. The small box marked "liquor cabinet."

Inside is a bottle of watermelon-flavored vodka, vermouth, and for some godforsaken reason, cinnamon-flavored whiskey. As a mostly non-drinker, I can't say I always made the best choices when perusing the liquor store.

I set all three bottles on the counter and spread my hands out. "Pick your poison."

"No thanks. I don't drink," Stone says, shaking his head.

"Fair enough. I can't say I was thrilled with the selection here either. The hostess here sucks," I say, walking around the counter and facing him. "So spill, then."

"You're not gonna like it," he whispers.

"Well, gee, it's almost like I coulda guessed that by the lost puppy dog look you've had since I got home. Does this have something to do with the invocation?" I ask, pressing on the question lingering in my mind. Did I actually hear what I thought I heard? Or am I delusional and need to be checked out.

His eyes are emerald saucers and his mouth gapes open. "Invocation?"

I've been with enough lying mofo's to know when the question shot across the bow has hit its mark. I plant a hand on my hip. "Yeah."

"How'd you—? The full moon," he says, nodding as if that's an actual valid reason.

"If you're trying to say this is a hormonal woman thing..." I begin, ready to break out some attitude.

He shakes his head, holding his hands out in front of him. "No, not that. Look, Ella, what I'm about to tell you is going to flip your world upside down. I need to know that you can handle it."

I narrow my eyes and jut out my chin. "I've been through hell and back, Stone. Nothing you can tell me is going to be worse than that." Even as I say it, my heart hammers traitorously in my chest.

He presses his lips tight and nods.

It takes him a minute to collect his thoughts and I cross my arms over my chest as I wait.

"Ella, you're gonna be a werewolf," Stone says. His voice is so low, I'm surprised I even made out a word of it.

My mind starts to cartwheel into the realms of *why can't I attract someone into my life who's just normal?*

I nearly burst into laughter. "Get the fuck out. Am I being videotaped for America's most gullible women or something?" I glance around the kitchen for some sort of hidden video device.

"Who says videotaped anymore?" Asher mumbles under his breath as he enters the kitchen. He meanders over to the fridge for a sec, opens it, and closes it instantly. He must have forgotten we haven't been to the grocery store yet.

"Quiet you," I say, holding up an index finger like I'm about to dive into a diatribe of *back in my day*.

When I turn back to Stone, he's not laughing. If anything, his demeanor has shifted further down the desperate dude path.

"This isn't a joke. Doug—when he was trapped—he bit you, right?" Stone says, his voice still a low rumble.

"Yeah, that guy bit her. We kept telling her to get it checked out, but she doesn't listen so..." Asher says, spinning various boxes as he hunts for potential snacks.

"First of all, it's fine. Secondly, we've already had a traumatic couple of days, thanks. It hasn't really been on my mind," I spit back.

"It wouldn't matter anyway. They wouldn't find anything," Stone says. "Ella, please, this is important."

"What's important?" Avery asks, entering the kitchen. She meanders over to her brother, eyeing the contents of the box he's rooting around in. She grabs a handful of Fruit by the Foot and unwraps one.

"Then be serious," I say, shaking my head.

He pinches the bridge of his nose and takes a slow deliberate breath. "We don't have time for this."

"Then stop wasting—"

Suddenly, the energy of the room rises, like an intense static electricity about to be unleashed. The hairs on my arms, neck, and head, all stand on end.

Before my eyes—no, not even that—in the blink of an eye, Stone goes from standing before me in a pair of swim trunks to the largest white wolf I've ever seen. Only, it's not the first time I've seen this wolf.

I take a giant step back and shriek, "Fuck me. What in the actual?"

CHAPTER 18

DESTINED FOR MORE

My heart stops beating—at least, that's how it feels. I scramble backward, try to hop up onto the countertop, but misjudge its height, and end up sliding right back to the floor super gracefully. If by graceful I mean an elephant tap-dancing.

I must be outta my goddamn mind.

Am I dreaming?

Whatever the fuck this is, it's not reality. It can't be.

I turn to the kids. "What the hell was in that sushi?"

Their wide eyes and slacked jaws tell me all I need to know. This is a shared delusion. And a surprise one at that.

"Mom, he j-just—" Avery stumbles over her words as she points. Her finger quivers in the motion.

"He's a werewolf," Asher breathes. There's a hint of reverence in the final word, though, and it's enough to make me lose my shit.

My head snaps to Asher. "Don't be ridiculous. He can't be a—"

The white wolf edges forward, snapping out a bark.

I clutch the counter behind me and swallow hard. My knees suddenly feel weak.

Holy shit, he's intense.

"He sure seems like he's agreeing with Asher," Avery squeaks.

The kids are right. You can feel the truth in it. Can't you?

The thoughts intrude my mind and I return my gaze to Stone's...*wolf*. His green eyes are trained on me as if expecting me to say something.

I run my hands over my face. "This can't be happening. *Normal*. I just wanted a normal life. I'm done with the drama. Is that really too much to ask?"

Normal is overrated. You're destined for more.

I ball my hands into fists and snap, "Would you stop that?"

"Stop what?" Asher asks, grabbing hold of Avery and keeping her close. I don't know who he's more anxious of—the wolf or me.

I blink rapidly from him and Avery, then back to the wolf. "I just—"

Without another word, I turn on my heel, leaving

the kitchen entirely. For whatever reason, I have no worry whatsoever that the kids are in danger. Stone has already proven as much.

"This can't be real," I mutter to myself but something inside me is ringing true.

Granted a grown-ass man just turned into an enormous white wolf, so it's a little hard at this point to claim ignorance. Insanity, though... *Oh yeah.* I must have that in spades.

I head straight up the stairs, going to where I'd typically go when I needed a quiet moment to think: *my bedroom.*

However, hot on my heels is the white wolf, and I know this crazy train is only beginning if I allow him anywhere near me.

Fuck my life.

When I reach my bedroom, I'm momentarily taken aback when there's furniture and a buttload of boxes in the room. Nothing is set up where I want it, but at least I have a bed, I guess.

I spin around, expecting to slam the door to keep out the wolf, but instead, a tattooed arm attached to a strong hand keeps it from closing.

Stone steps into my bedroom buck ass naked and looking like some sort of Greek God here to claim a reckoning.

I suck in a quick breath and force my eyes upward to meet his, even though I'd *really* like to let my gaze wander.

A small smirk tugs at his lips but he continues into the room like it's perfectly normal to walk around with his bits open airing it around a total stranger. Well, a *mostly* stranger.

"Um, not sure if you're aware, but..." I raise a shaky pointer finger, ignoring the way my heart hammers in my chest and my lady bits tingle, "you're missing your attire."

He glances down, then shrugs. "A side effect, as it happens. Clothing can't survive the shift."

The word *shift* jangles inside my head. Nothing about it connects with anything resembling reality. Yet, a part of me nods in agreement. Like that sentence makes total sense.

"Well, I'd offer you some manly clothes, but I burned anything from my ex, so..." My voice trails off. "Pretty sure Asher isn't even close to your...er..." I glance at the ceiling and mutter, "size."

Christ, why does he have to be so hot?

Mental note... Call Denise to fill her in on this one. She won't believe me.

"Who's Denise?" Stone asks, continuing to prowl forward.

My gaze snaps to his. "What?"

Stone chuckles. "You haven't figured it out yet. Have you? We're connected telepathically. I can hear your thoughts and you can hear mine."

"We are? Like, you and me? How?" I sputter. This whole thing is getting weirder and weirder.

His eyebrows tug in and a hint of pain skitters across his face. "The whole pack. It's our primary communication mode when we're in wolf form, but it's with us all the time. Well, most of us."

I quirk an eyebrow. "Most?"

His lips press tight. "There's a lot to learn and I don't want to inundate you with the politics of it all yet. Right now, I need to get you up to speed because there's a challenge against your claim," Stone says.

I hold up a hand. If there's one thing this mom can suss out, it's a partial truth. "Whoa, whoa. Back up. I don't give a shit about politics, but it seems to me there's something important that you're skirting around here. Spill it."

Stone inhales sharply, almost wincing. After a beat, he nods and continues, "Doug was the Alpha of our pack. He bit you—making you his chosen Alpha successor. There's also a Beta—the second in command. His name is Silas and he's...not happy with the state of affairs. He's the one who is challenging your claim."

Narrowing my gaze, I cross my arms. "And what does this make you?"

His lips pinch tight and he whispers, "Nothing much. I'm considered an Omega."

I drop my hands. "Okay, now I know you're making this shit up. Omega? What does that even mean?"

"It means the outcast. Not every pack has one, but

Silas—" Stone crumples his face, running his fingertips over his forehead.

"If you're the outcast... Is that what you meant about most of us?" I ask, trying to piece things together.

He nods. "My connection with the pack was somewhat severed. But because of my connection to Clementine, I can still hear at times. Not as well. It usually takes close proximity," he says, shrugging. "And, as it happens, you haven't learned how to shut us out when you want to yet."

I blink wildly and walk over to the window. "Does that mean *everyone* can hear my thoughts?"

This whole thing is running away with the crazy and I'm not entirely sure I'm buying any of it.

"I don't know," he says, his eyebrows skirting his hairline. "But it's possible."

"Great." I roll my eyes. Sighing heavily, I pinch the bridge of my nose. "Okay, say I believe you—what's wrong with just letting this guy Silas take over. I mean, he's gotta be poised as a better leader than I'll be. I mean, come on—some newbie woman leading the...*group*." I'm not prepared to say words like *werewolf* and *pack* just yet. "I'm no enterprise expert, but even I know that installing a leader who doesn't know two things about the people they're supposed to lead is a bad idea."

Stone steps up beside me, shaking his head. "You don't get it. Werewolves don't care about that. Not when the Alpha has chosen. It's an accepted fact. And Silas is bad news. If he gets his way, he'll turn the Black Crater Pack into something unrecognizable."

"I know change is hard, but come on…" I begin.

"He believes we're the dominant species—that humans should be subservient to us…" His voice trails off and his jaw sets. "His vision won't be pretty. It could mean war with the human world."

Yeesh, that does sound bad.

"If he's such bad news, why was he second in command?" I say, quirking an eyebrow.

"Because Doug had a big heart and thought it was best to keep Silas close. Silas should have been the one exiled. Instead, Doug was misguided and it got him killed," Stone grounds out. "It's one thing to betray me, but it's another thing to murder his Alpha."

"Are you saying what I think you're saying?" I say, inhaling sharply.

Stone nods, his eyes glinting dangerously. "Probably."

"Silas was the one who ran Doug off the road?" I spit out.

"Yeah," he says, his face darkening. "We can't let him get his hands on the pack. Doug knew it, too. It's why he did what he did, Ella. It has to be. I've been over that day in my mind a thousand different times, a thousand different ways and I keep coming back to the same conclusion. He saw something in you—a heart, compassion—everything he knew the pack needs to continue on the right path. Something Silas is obviously incapable of. Doug risked everything to pass the torch onto you. You have to pick it up."

"I didn't ask for this. I didn't want any of it—" I say, backing away. It's still so unbelievable.

"I know you didn't but it's the hand you've been dealt, regardless. You can't escape it. You can't change it—the shift is imminent. You can feel the pull, can't you?" Stone asks, his index finger pointing out the window toward the rising moon.

He wasn't wrong. There was something—an antsy sort of energy that made my skin tingle and my blood hum. And no, it wasn't just his naked body being so close to me. Though, I'd have no doubt he'd have a similar effect if things were different.

A sad smile flits across his face and he takes another step forward, placing his hands on my upper arms. "The pack needs you, Ella. I understand if this is scary but—"

"I'm not scared. Fuck that guy. He's an asshole that should be put in his place," I spit. "I'm just not sure I'm the person to do that."

"There's only one way to find out."

I hold his gaze for a moment, weighing my options. If what Stone says is true, this Silas guy has already killed the sitting Alpha. Someone I'm coming to understand has some power in the pack. He's also come at me and my family. Even if I wanted to walk away, he's made it personal.

My children didn't deserve the kind of fucked up day we've had. If anything, they deserve to feel safe, loved, and in control of their destinies.

I close my eyes, weighing my options.

"Ella, I'll help you. You won't have to do this alone," Stone whispers.

When I open my eyes, his green gaze pleads with me.

Exhaling slowly, I say, "What do I have to do?"

CHAPTER 19
FOCUS ON ME

ELLA

Worry lines mar Stone's face and he takes a slow, deliberate breath before saying, "You'll need to prove your dominance over Silas."

I narrow my gaze. "Which means what, exactly?"

He scratches at the side of his temple. "This is so awkward to describe to someone who's never been in this world."

"Believe me, it's way worse from the receiving end," I mutter.

His eyebrows rise and he nods. "I suppose that would be true. Look, maybe this is the easiest way to describe it. Have you ever seen dogs fight?"

I shrug. "Sure."

The fact that we're having a conversation about dog fights in relationship to something I may need to do very soon is incredibly wiggy, but I keep my eyes trained on him.

"It's sort of the same concept. The two of you will shift and, for lack of better terms, *fight*," he says.

Panic suddenly claws at my insides. "Like, to the death?"

Again, worry and concern cross his features, but he shakes his head. "No, it shouldn't come to that. Not with the pack watching."

"Oh, great. So there'll be an audience," I say, walking away from the window and taking a seat on the edge of my bed. I drop my head in my hands to avoid direct line of sight with his midsection.

Stone walks over to me, taking a seat beside me. Thankfully, he crosses his arms over his lap. "That audience is the one thing that could keep you alive, Ella. We both know Silas doesn't fight fair. There's a reason Silas went after Doug outside of our territory—and in human form."

Stone's words send a chill down my spine. I hadn't even thought about this being a one-way ticket sort of endeavor.

Fuck.

"Ella, I'll do everything I can to keep you safe," he whispers. His words take on a haunting quality and I glance over my shoulder at him. "I failed Doug. I won't fail you, too."

I snicker. "Look at us. Some great leadership going on here. A clueless Alpha and her outcast."

A smile plays at Stone's lips and he quirks an eyebrow. "*Her* outcast?"

"You know what I mean," I say, feeling the heat rush to my face.

His emerald eyes lock with mine and I fight the urge to look away since my gaze would probably land on the forbidden zone.

"God, none of this makes sense—and makes total sense. It's messing with my head," I say, brushing my fingertips against my eyebrow.

"Ella, it's been a long time since I had hope for the Black Crater pack. When I first realized Doug was dead—I honestly thought I'd have to get to Clementine and we'd run. But then I saw you...and I just *knew*. You're going to be an incredible leader," he says.

His words hold so much conviction, I'm forced to look into his expectant gaze again.

He holds out his arm, brushing a stray hair behind my ear. The movement, combined with his words, makes my insides flutter.

As if in slow motion, he leans in, bending toward me. His lips brush mine, igniting my nerve-endings with anticipation. He smells like the forest after a good rain and I sink into his kiss, wanting more than anything something that feels safe.

However, as quickly as it began, he pulls back. "I'm sorry—I shouldn't have..." his words soften until they're a whisper.

I blink back my surprise, trying to get a wrangle on my feelings.

I wanted him to kiss me... Right?

My body says unequivocally *yes*. But my mind is rampaging on a tangent about my insanity.

Glancing at him, I get an eyeful of his body's reaction as well and it sparks another burst of desire. I stand up quickly, swallowing hard.

Holy shit.

"Mom, someone's at the door," Asher says from the doorway. Thankfully, from his angle, he can only see Stone's back. Goodness knows I don't need to have a conversation about why there's a naked man with a massive erection hanging out in my bedroom.

Confusion consumes me, but before I can say a word, Stone cuts in, "It's Clementine."

"How do you—?" I begin, but nod to myself, "Right." I don't know how I'm meant to get used to this telepathy thing. "Send her up."

Asher nods and disappears.

I can only imagine the conversations I'm going to have to endure with the kids. They must be so freaked out right now.

Stone stands up, walking over to me. His erection has tamed itself, but I suck in a breath anyway at his proximity. I don't know what it is about his presence but he brings out something in me—*something primal*. It's like nothing I've ever felt in my forty-two years on this planet and the more I catch glimpses of it, the more I want it.

But the intensity of it is borderline scary.

He places a hand on my shoulder. "I'm—"

"For Christ's sake, put some clothes on. Can't you see you're making her uncomfortable?" Clementine says, walking into the bedroom like it's the hundredth time. She shoves a pair of swim trunks at him, then she catches my eye and the tiniest smirk graces her lips. Thank the lord, she doesn't call me out on my obvious attraction to her brother. She doesn't even give Stone a second glance. Instead, she spins back the way she came. "So, since I get to hang out here, anyone wanna introduce me to the kids?"

Stone steps into his swim trunks, blissfully ending the eyeful ready to set me up in flames. It's bad enough he's hot from the waist up.

"What are you talking about?"

"You can't bring the kids to the grove and I'll be damned if we leave your kids unprotected. Silas has already sent people unconnected to the pack to take you out. I refuse to let that be an option again," Stone says, his words more of a growl. "I asked her to stay with them."

"Are you sure?" I ask, turning to them both.

Clementine shrugs. "I'm good."

"There's no one I trust more," Stone answers.

"Awww, thanks, little brother," she says, reaching forward and messing up his hair.

Funnily enough, his wild hair just makes him hotter.

"Boy, you've got it bad," Clementine mutters, shooting me a knowing glance.

I shake my head. "I don't know what you mean."

"Oookay," she says, nodding. But she held that 'o' a bit too long for my liking.

Stone takes a slow, deep breath, then walks to the doorway. "Come on. We'll need to get going. The pack's expecting us."

"Hold up. This is all happening kinda fast. I mean, can't I just have a few minutes to—" I begin.

"Ella, you'll do great," Clementine says, her green eyes warm as she pats my back and gently pushes me toward her brother.

"But what if—"

Stone's broad shoulders are framed by the doorway as he waits for me. "I know you didn't ask for this, but it's your destiny now. All you have to do is be open."

"Agreed," Clementine says from behind my shoulder.

Without another word, he walks out, vanishing into the hallway. I follow after him.

He's right. Delaying the inevitable has never kept people safe. If anything, it's always been a hindrance, not a help.

"Mom, are you...okay?" Avery asks, her brown eyes wide with worry.

I reach out for her, tugging her into a quick hug. "I'm good, sweetie. I'm just..." My voice trails off. How do I expect them to believe all of this when I barely do?

"You have to go, don't you?" Asher says, ever the astute one.

I reach out, pulling him in, too. "For a bit."

"Lucky for you, you get to be stuck with me," Clementine says, jabbing her thumbs to her shoulders.

I chuckle softly under my breath and twist the kids to face her. "Kids, this is Clementine. She's Stone's sister."

Recognition creeps up Asher's face. "You're the wife to the guy in the ravine."

Sadness washes over her features but as quickly as they arise, she pushes them back. "That's me."

"I'm so sorry about your husband," Avery says, her lips twisting slightly to the side.

"Thank you. Boy, you sure have some thoughtful kids, Ella," Clementine says, smiling softly.

My heart beams. As much as they can fight like cats and dogs, they do have their hearts in the right place. Thank God for that.

"We need to go," Stone whispers.

"How long will this last?" I ask, meeting his intense stare.

He sighs. "As long as it takes for one of you to submit."

"So, not long then," I say, chuckling darkly.

"I think you're gonna surprise yourself," Stone offers.

"Yeah, well..." I turn to face the kids. "Guys, I want you to keep me posted. Text me or call. If anything happens, your asses better call me the second before."

"How does that work?" Avery asks, her features tight.

"Stay alert and trust no one," I say, lowering my voice. I trust Clementine, otherwise, I wouldn't be willing to leave. But that doesn't mean they shouldn't stay on their toes.

Asher reaches out, wrapping his arms around my neck. Avery follows suit, wrapping her arms around my waist. I cling to them, knowing how significant this moment is.

If shit went sideways, it could be the last time they see me.

Oh, hell no. I refuse to let that be the reality.

I didn't escape one horrible situation only to thrust them back into that life.

I'll do whatever it takes to keep them safe. From their past—and anything that goes howl in the middle of the night.

With a final breath, I let go and walk out of the house. I don't bother grabbing anything but my car keys.

Stone follows out after me.

"Give 'em hell," Clementine calls out to us from my front door.

I march over to my Highlander and get inside. Within seconds, Stone takes up residence in the seat beside me.

"All right... where to?" I say, starting the vehicle and shifting into reverse.

"Head north off the highway. I'll get you as close as I can. Then we'll have to make the rest of the journey on foot," he says, snapping his seatbelt into place.

"Super," I mutter.

The drive is a long, quiet journey. Stone is silent, letting me sort through my thoughts on my own.

There's so much to parse apart.

Between the revelation that I was bit by a werewolf and about to become his heir—or successor—whatever... and the crazy feelings surfacing for Stone, I don't know which way is up. It's like I've dropped into a surreal world where everything is upside down.

"It won't always feel this strange, you know," Stone says, his gaze out into the treeline.

I snicker under my breath. "Easy for you to say."

He glances at me over his shoulder. "I wasn't looking for anyone either."

His confession invokes goosebumps across my skin. I chance a quick look his way. "What does that mean?"

He clears his throat. "When I was cast out of the pack, I knew I probably wouldn't ever—" His gaze drops to his lap, then drifts back out his window. "Finding a mate as the Omega is unheard of."

"Are you saying you can't have sex?" I say, my eyes wide. "Is that what you mean?"

He chuckles. "No, not entirely."

"Then what?" I sneak another quick glance.

He runs his fingertips across the space just beneath his lower lip. "It's complicated."

"Uncomplicate it."

His eyes narrow and he turns to face me. "I think we should keep things simple for now."

"Oh." I blink hard at him. "Okay."

Disappointment rolls through me and I return my gaze to the road, fighting back the anxiety his words invoke.

"We're here," he says. "Park over there." He points to the right, in a small opening between trees.

I do as he commands.

"Now we walk," he says, opening his door and hopping out.

I take a beat, staring at the steering wheel. Before I can get to my handle, Stone opens my door for me.

"Thanks," I mutter, my heart rate suddenly climbing into dangerous zones.

"You'll be okay," he says, his voice is strong and assured as he places his hand on my back, guiding me into the woods.

After a good twenty-minute hike in the densest forest I've ever meandered through, we come upon a large stone circle that looks like it was pulled straight out of a fantasy novel. Moss covers the stones and the bright light of the nearly full moon beats down on the space.

Stone leads me into its center and all I can do is stare in awe.

It's beautiful—*damn near magical.*

Suddenly, movement pulls me from my reverie and I realize we're surrounded.

Wolves of all shapes and sizes descend from the outer edges of the forest.

There are so many of them in this one location and it makes my insides turn to mush.

What if they have this all wrong? What if I'm not one of them? What if...

Look at her. She's so weak.

This won't last more than a few minutes.

I hope Stone isn't playing us.

She won't last ten seconds...

My heart leaps into my throat. They're all voicing the same concerns rolling through my head.

Stone's voice cuts through the noise, rising like an island in the middle of a storming sea. *Don't worry about them. Just focus on me.*

CHAPTER 20

PERFORMANCE ANXIETY

ELLA

I turn to face Stone, but his discerning gaze is cast out over the wolves who have begun to circle us. His focus is hardcore, though—as if he's searching for someone in specific.

I suppose he is.

Suddenly, the pack of wolves parts, and an enormous black wolf slinks forward. Even in the low light of the moonlit evening, I can tell his eyes are blood red. They practically glow with malice and when they lock with mine, his stare sends chills straight down my spine.

I suck in a quick breath and take a small step backward.

Don't show that he intimidates you. It looks like weakness to the pack. Stone's words have an edge to them but make sense nonetheless.

I inhale sharply, thrusting my chin up and shoulders back. I've had to deal with asshat men thinking they can own my thoughts and actions before. I was done with it the minute I signed for a divorce. I'll be damned if I let another one try.

Wolf or human—Silas is still a guy trying to put a woman down.

Fuck that.

"Silas, I presume," I say, planting a hand on my hip and channeling my inner bitch. Denise would be proud.

He prowls forward, circling me and Stone counter-clockwise.

When he makes a full circumference, I quirk an eyebrow and try to play down my fear. "To be honest, I thought you'd be bigger."

The enormous wolf growls, its snout pulling back and baring the kind of teeth that go on for miles.

If there was any question whether or not he understood my words in wolf form, there isn't now.

"So, I thought I was brought here to talk business. How are we meant to do that when everyone's all fur and snarls?" I ask, eyeing all of the other wolves.

I know damn well *talking* isn't on the agenda. I might not have dogs, but I do know how they determine rank. Even I'm not that sheltered.

The surreal fact that I'm standing in the middle of a forest-hidden stone sanctuary, surrounded by wolves—no, *werewolves*—isn't lost on me, either. But if there's one thing I've been good at, it's dealing with a world of weird.

I mean, I have two teenagers.

Stone nods. "Ella's right. As a Bitten, she's at a disadvantage. She doesn't know our rules, or—"

And yet, even a Bitten should have a link with their pack. Silas's thoughts invade my mind, but I ignore them. If he doesn't know I can hear him, that could be an advantage later on.

The black wolf shivers, like a dog shaking away the rain, but in the motion, he transforms into a muscular man crouched down in a superhero-type stance. Silas has a deep tan that defines his muscles and the same crescent moon tribal tattoo that Stone has etched on his chest is painted across his left shoulder. It must be a symbol of the pack.

He stands up and, just like Stone, Silas has zero fucks to give about being naked in front of an audience.

I sigh, crossing my arms over my torso and refusing to divert my gaze. At least Stone's little stunt at the house prepared me a bit for this.

Silas's mouth slides into a smirk and he walks forward with an air of confident arrogance. It's true, he has an advantage over me. He's an enormous, six-foot-something dude with badass muscles and a menacing black crew cut, and tattoos splattered all over the place. Plus, he has the bonus of knowing everyone here and the rules in place with this band of mythical creatures.

I, on the other hand... Yeah, I'm not even sure this is real or if I died when those goons entered my home earlier.

All I know is, whatever is happening to me feels inevitable...*and important.* Being here, in this place has set my very being humming—*vibrating.* It's almost as good as sex and whatever it is, I could get used to it.

"She doesn't look like much," Silas says, his words slithering out of his mouth like the snake I've already taken him for.

"Awww, did I hurt your feelings when I said you weren't very big? Well, if it's any consolation, now I can say that goes for more ways than one," I say, without properly thinking through my words.

Before I have time to react, Silas is on me. His enormous hand grasps around my throat and squeezes. My breath catches in my throat and my vision swims. Instinctively, my hands rise and I claw to get Silas off, but he lifts me straight off the ground with one hand.

Stars burst across my sight, but I somehow manage to swing my right foot back and land it right in his exposed groin. Instantly, I drop to the stone floor, crumpling into a heap and gasping for air.

When I manage to look up, standing between me and Silas is the white wolf. Stone's hackles are raised and he snaps his teeth, forcing Silas to take a tiny concession backward as he gropes at himself, pulling in jagged breaths of his own.

Fucker.

"Stop," a woman says off to my right. She stalks toward us in her birthday suit, her lean body in the kind of shape I would have killed for twenty years ago. She, too, has the crescent tattoo, but it's placed above her left hip. "The Law of the Bitten is clear. Until the Alpha manages their first shift, no harm can come to them. Anyone who tries would be exiled."

"Stay out of this, Marta," Silas mutters, dropping his hands from himself and rounding on her.

"If you challenge her, it must be as a wolf and she must accept," she demands, tipping her chin up and going toe to toe with him. Her blond hair blows in the breeze, adding to a level of tension between them.

Stone snarls his agreement.

Clearing my throat, I shake my head and rise. *Wow. I mean, I knew about toxic masculinity, but his ego is fragile as fuck. It must be hell having to keep that thing stroked.*

"What did you say?" Silas says, his eyebrows darkening his face.

My eyes widen and I look around. "I didn't say anything." Out loud...*oh, fuck.*

As entertaining as it is to watch you, Ella, you have to remember he's not stable. Don't provoke him. Not yet. Stone's thoughts invade my mind and he chances a glance in my direction.

I shrug in return. I make no promises there. But dang, I need to learn how to direct thoughts at people instead of broadcasting them to the whole world. So much for keeping the element of surprise.

I swear I feel his exasperation roll off him as he returns his attention to Silas.

"You need to learn your place," Silas spits, throwing his shoulders back and popping his pecs like it's gonna impress anyone but him.

I step forward. "See, I might be new here...but as I understand it, that's ironic, seeing as you were deliberately cockblocked and I'm meant to be your boss or whatever."

Marta snickers softly, but falls back in line with the others.

I like her. She's got fire. Her thoughts reach me and somehow I know they're hers and no one else's.

More like stupidity.

Yeah, but look at her. There's nothing to her. Silas could take her with his eyes closed.

I bet her wolf is tiny.

The new thoughts jumble together and I can't pinpoint their sources, despite eyeing the wolves around us. While I can hear them, it's like being in a crowded room where everyone is talking all at once. You can make out conversations, but who knows who says what.

It's strange how some thoughts are clear—like Stone's and Marta's—while others are hazy and nebulous.

What's up with that?

"You've got a mouth on you. I can think of better uses for it," Silas grounds out.

Stone snaps his jaws at Silas, evidently as unamused as I am with that one.

I narrow my gaze, but keep my mouth shut this time. I know when enough innuendo is enough and he's pushing things too far. The last thing I need is for him to go off half-cocked.

Despite myself, I snicker at that last thought, then hope like hell that it didn't broadcast.

"What's so funny? Like the idea, do you?" Silas says, his dark eyes flashing. They're not nearly as scary as his wolf's glowing red gaze, but they speak of terrible deeds nonetheless.

Thank God, he didn't hear it.

Stone's right. This asshole has to go down.

"I was just wondering... Are we gonna do this thing? Or are you gonna talk me to death?" I say, stepping forward and petting Stone between the ears. I have no idea if he likes that kind of gesture or thinks it's condescending, but I continue forward anyway.

"Finally," Silas says, his voice a barely tamed growl.

Before I can say anything else, Silas shudders, transforming into his wolf again.

Panic suddenly floods my system.

Shit. Why didn't we do a trial run of this?

I turn my wild gaze to Stone, who takes up residence on my left-hand side.

It's as easy as breathing. Don't worry. Just see yourself shifting into your wolf—lean into the feeling of it and let go. Stone says, his eyes trained on Silas.

"Oh, yeah. Easy," I mutter. My heartbeat hammers in my chest, and my insides feel like they've turned to mush.

Now is not a great time to lose my lunch.

And awesome, I think I need to pee. Goddamn tiny "mom" bladder.

Relax. The more you panic, the more you force your wolf away.

"For fucksake, you try not to panic when you're expected to do something you don't even know you can do in front of a shit-ton of—" I cut off my words, flitting my gaze around the circle.

On top of it, even if I do shift, all it means is I'm going to be in a battle with the enormous menace circling me like I'm his next meal.

Fuck my life.

Shift already. The sooner we end this joke, the better. Silas's words invade my mind like a dagger.

"Hey," I say, indignant. "This isn't my ideal life, either, buddy."

Silas lunges forward snapping his jaws in my direction.

Everything inside me is screaming—like it knows what it wants to do, what it needs to do...but it can't. Or won't.

Instead, I feel like I'm being split apart—my mind and body fracturing like a pane of glass.

Stop fighting the shift, Ella. Just let go. Stone says, worry filtering from his mind to mine.

"I know. It's just—" I say, shaking my head. I can feel it, my body wants desperately to do something my logical mind can't seem to grasp. The war waging internally is enough to make me buckle over. I drop to my knees, needing to be closer to the ground as if somehow that's going to help me.

Look, she can't even shift. She's no Alpha. Someone to the right of Marta scoffs.

I knew this was all bullshit. I bet Stone made it up to get back at Silas.

He should just end her now.

But other thoughts mingle with those.

Why isn't she shifting?

Come on...you can do it.

Relax into it. You'll love the feeling.

I glance around, searching for their source. As I focus on them, it's like a soft white light draws my attention to the owners of those happier thoughts.

Your connection to the pack is growing stronger. Forget the naysayers. Lean into those who need you. Who already favor you. Stone says.

I close my eyes, trying to do what he said—lean

into the feeling and let go. For a moment, I drop into that sensation, but the horrible realization of what comes next takes me straight out of the moment.

"I can't do it," I finally say, wiping beads of sweat from my forehead.

Silas howls and the sound practically rips my soul from my body. His supporters join in and their combined sound is damned near haunting.

Then, without warning, Silas leaps from his spot. His black paws slam into my right shoulder, knocking me off-center. I fly backward, smacking my head on the rocks. Again, stars burst through my vision and I try quickly to blink away their effects.

Thankfully, Stone intercepts. His jaws latch onto the scruff of Silas's neck and he pulls him off me in the same fluid motion. The two of them tussle—nothing more than snapping jaws and growls.

Marta, still in human form, steps into the arena— at least, that's what it feels like—acting as the referee between the two of them.

"Back off, Silas. You know the rules. She has until the full moon to make the shift," Marta says, again speaking up for me. "Postpone this until she can manage it."

Stone is still attached to Silas's neck, but they both stop in mid-attack as if their mom just called them out. After a moment, Silas shakes out of Stone's grasp and glances into the mix of wolves behind him. Two wolves step out of the crowd and instantly, I get the impression it was a silent command.

Then, Silas turns back to me, his red eyes glowing as his thoughts echo out louder than any other I've experienced. *Tomorrow night, you're going down, mouthy. Lock them both up.*

CHAPTER 21

I SHOULDN'T EVEN BE HERE

ELLA

The two wolves Silas signaled immediately transform into their human versions. Of course, they're both the size of Fort Knox, too. In a coordinated effort, one grabs hold of Stone by the scruff of his neck, while the other one lunges at me.

Thankfully, I've been in enough bars throughout my years to see that kind of grab a mile off. I sidestep, slapping his hand away. "Hey—hands off."

"Without witnessing your shift, we can't risk letting you out of our sight," Silas says, also transforming back into a human. "If you're not one of us, you could expose us to the world."

"I think you do that well enough for yourself," I mutter, waving my index finger up and down, suggesting his person.

I can tell you one thing, I've never been

surrounded by this many naked guys and it's putting me on edge. And not in a good way.

Marta steps forward again, as do two other women. One is short, with curly brown hair that reaches to the middle of her back. I gotta hand it to her, though. She got enough muscles to compete in a Ms. Universe contest or whatever those things are called. The other woman is no more than twenty, with big blue eyes and jet black hair. She's also built and I'm getting the sneaky suspicion being a werewolf requires a certain amount of mass.

Joke's on them with me, that's for damn sure.

However, despite having this bizarre naked train balance out with more women, it still does nothing to ease my anxiety.

There's no way in hell I'll ever get used to this.

"Silas is right. It's best to stay with us until our Alpha is chosen," Marta says. Evidently, she's a stickler for all the rules.

"Dammit, I have kids—" I begin, glaring at Silas. "I don't want them left alone overnight. He's already attacked my family once. I won't let that happen again."

Marta and the other women turn their questioning gaze to Silas.

"Is this true?" the blue-eyed one asks.

Silas crosses his bulky arms over his chest and presses his lips tight. From what I can tell, it's his way of pleading the fifth.

Stone shifts out of his wolf form, shrugging from beneath Fort Knox number one's grip. He bats the guy's arm away and takes a step in my direction. "Ella's right. I witnessed the whole thing myself."

"Witnessed it? He *ended* it," I practically shout. "If it wasn't for Stone, my kids and I would be dead."

A murmur rolls through the crowd. People and wolves alike shift in their spots.

I catch snippets of thoughts, but each fly by too fast for me to latch onto.

"Lies," Silas spits, but his expression holds too much pride. Anyone with eyeballs can see it.

"Her attackers admitted to it," Stone grounds out, stepping into Silas's space. "I guess you get what you pay for. Humans break rank easily."

Stone turns to everyone, his chest puffed up, and fists clenched at his side. "Why do you think I invoked the Law of the Bitten? If I hadn't, who knows what Silas had planned next. He was hoping no one knew of her."

"What? Are you certain?" The brown-haired woman exclaims.

More wolves shift into their human forms—men and women alike. Many faces are full of alarm, while others only hold malice for Stone. I make a mental note. They must be Silas's crew.

"Why is anyone believing a word from this piece of shit? Do none of you remember what he is?" Silas snarls, holding his arms out wide as he circles on his spot. "He's the *Omega* for a reason. You'd all do well to remember that."

"Yeah, a great reason. It was *your* reason," Stone grounds out, his jaw tightening.

"Enough. This will resolve itself when the two claims are challenged tomorrow and a winner is declared," Marta says, commanding the voice of authority here. For some reason, those around her listen and if I survive this whole thing, I'll have to figure out why. She turns to me. "Ella, you can return home, but you'll need to be kept under a watchful eye. We'll need you back here by sundown."

"Clementine and I will do it," Stone offers.

I breathe a sigh of relief. The two of them I can handle.

"Are you certain Clementine will agree? I can't help but notice she's not even here," Marta asks, her expression skeptical.

"Who do you think is protecting Ella's kids right now?" Stone says, matter-of-factly.

"Really?" Marta says, surprise painted across her features as she turns to me.

"Yeah, and if you think I'm gonna repay her kindness by making her spend the night at my house alone with my two scared teenagers, you're all cracked," I spit.

Marta narrows her gaze for a moment, then nods. "It is done. Go, but be back by sundown."

A rumble echoes from Silas's chest and he clenches his fists. "She should be locked up."

"As challenger, you have no right to dictate anything, Silas," Marta announces.

"But I am your Beta—"

Marta steps into his space, clearly not frightened by the dominance he commands. "You forfeited that role the moment you challenged a Bitten. You are both in limbo until our Alpha is chosen. As Beta, you should have known these rules."

Stone smirks, quickly glancing in my direction.

If I had to wager a guess, Stone was *well aware* of this little rule. And he also knew Silas wasn't in the know.

"Speaking of Silas," Stone says, jabbing a thumb in his direction. "If Ella is to be watched, he should also be monitored. Who knows what he and his crew could conspire if left unattended."

"Agreed. I will see to it myself," Marta offers with a brisk nod. "I'd like to get to the bottom of your claim that he had Ella attacked." Her golden eyes flit to Silas, who returns her stare by throwing daggers with his eyes.

There's no love lost there, that's for sure.

Stone exhales, shooting me another sideways glance. His demeanor softens and it's pretty clear he trusts Marta to take care of business there.

Without any more discussion, the wolves disperse,

vanishing into the darkness beyond the stone circle. Besides Stone and I, anyone still in human form shifts into their wolf. I watch them with a new sense of wonder and awe. This place—this situation is surreal as fuck, but the more I'm surrounded by it, the more it feels...*right.*

Within a matter of minutes, Stone and I are left alone in the middle of the circle.

Seriousness broods in his eyes as he steps toward me. My breath hitches and I keep my gaze locked on his, trying desperately to keep them north of his midsection.

"What happened? Why didn't you shift?" he asks, his voice just above a whisper. "I could feel your power rising. It should have happened."

I sigh, accidentally dropping my gaze to the ground. I zip it straight back to his face when I catch more than anticipated on the way down. Swallowing hard, I shake away the inklings of desire that roll through me. I seriously need to get better control of myself.

"I think it's because I don't know what to expect next," I admit.

"It's a weird sensation, but you'll get used to it..."

"No, I don't mean that, per se. Though, not knowing how isn't helping," I say, stepping away from him. "I mean, what can I do to protect myself from Silas, Stone? How do I come out on top of this? He has experience and size on his side. Who am I? I'm a suburban mom, for Christsake. I'm no one. I shouldn't even be here. Hell, I don't even know how any of them are taking me seriously."

I walk out of the stone circle, pinching the bridge of my nose.

"They're taking you seriously because they *feel* the truth in it. If I can, *they* can. And *suburban mom* may have been who you were before—but it's not all you are," Stone declares, just over my right shoulder. "Look, you're right. Silas has experience, but you have one thing he'll never have."

"And what's that?" I glance over my shoulder as I continue walking in the general direction we came from. "If you say boobs, so help me..."

He chuckles. "No, but now that you mention it..."

"Shut up," I fire back, fighting the smile trying to grapple its way to my lips.

He grabs hold of my wrist, halting my progress. "You have the power of *an Alpha*. Silas may be big and think he's all that, but he's no Alpha. With any kind of luck, he won't ever be. I don't—I guess I don't think anyone has properly explained what that means."

I turn to face him but tip my chin up toward the moon. Good god, how can anyone concentrate on a conversation when there's so much nudity going on?

Especially when it's been ages since I got laid and Stone has some insane sex appeal.

"Please tell me you have a change of clothes hidden in the trees somewhere," I mutter.

He huffs out a laugh. "Am I making you nervous?"

"No, but you're distracting as fuck and I think this conversation is serious and one I really need to understand." I continue looking at the moon, noticing the tiniest of slivers is still missing. I never noticed that before.

"Come on. My house isn't far from here. I'll get changed and we can talk like two *civilized* adults," he says, but amusement still plays at his tone.

"Sweet relief," I say, dropping my gaze out to the woods. "Which way again?"

"Close your eyes."

"Why?"

"Would you stop being such a skeptic for two minutes? Trust me," he mutters, careful to stay behind me.

"Fine." I close my eyes and wait.

"Inhale slowly and tell me what you sense."

I do as he asks, inhaling slowly through my nose. Almost instantly, a familiar scent—*one I'm beginning to associate with him*—filters into my awareness. It's the smell of the woods after a good rain, only it hasn't rained for days.

I turn my head and follow it.

"See, I knew you could do it," Stone says with a hint of pride in his tone. "Your senses are still heightening. It will take you a while to incorporate and catalog it all. But once you do, you'll wonder how you ever lived as a human."

"If I make it past tomorrow night," I whisper under my breath.

"You will."

I shake my head. "How can you sound so sure of that?"

"Because I refuse to accept anything else. The pack needs you and I think you need the pack."

My heart trips over itself but I keep on walking. It's obvious he cares so much about the pack, despite being the outcast. If I'd been shunned by my family, I would have said the hell with them and moved as far away as possible. Come to think of it, I kinda did.

"Stone, what happened between you and Silas?" I ask, knowing we still have a few minutes left before we're at the vehicle.

"What do you mean?"

"I *mean*," I say, drawing out the word, "what's the dealio between you and Silas? He's the reason you were ostracized, right?"

Silence expands between us for a second and I know he's not happy I brought this up.

"Yeah, you could say that," he mutters, his humor all but vanishing.

"So, wanna tell me about it?" I press. "If I'm gonna be the next Alpha, shouldn't I know?"

"There's not a helluva lot to tell. Silas wanted me out of the picture, so he found a way," Stone grounds out.

I nearly trip over a tree branch that grabs hold of

my shoelace, but Stone catches me by my upper arm, somehow managing to keep me upright.

"Please tell me I start getting better reflexes if I turn into a damn werewolf," I mutter.

"You will." He chuckles.

"Thank God."

A few minutes later, we reach the vehicle and I get into the driver's seat. Stone takes up his spot beside me and thankfully, in the darkness of the cab, it's easier to forget he's in the buff.

"Why did he want you out of the picture?" I ask, chancing a glance at him before we get out of here.

"Isn't it obvious?" Stone asks, quirking an eyebrow. "He's always had the ambition to take over the pack."

"And he couldn't do that with you around?" I ask, starting up the Highlander.

Stone shakes his head. "Nope."

"Why not?" I ask, searching his eyes.

Stone turns his gaze toward the window and sighs. "Because I was the Beta."

CHAPTER 22

RESURRECTION

STONE

S tone half expected Ella to be upset with him that he hadn't told her about his previous status sooner. But she had accepted it with grace. It was almost as if it made total sense to her.

However, she had fallen silent and her barrage of questions had ended. By that point, he was too scared to bring it back up. If she did, he knew the conversation would go sideways fast.

As it was, she barely spoke when they arrived at his home so he could change. She stayed in her vehicle, refusing to even come in.

To be fair, he was consumed by his thoughts. He wanted desperately to keep Ella and her kids safe, but he didn't understand where the intense pull was coming from. It didn't make sense.

He'd never felt this kind of connection to someone before. Even as Beta, when half the pack was vying to be his mate, he hadn't had any time for it. His focus was on the pack as a whole. Not the desires of the individual.

Hell, he fully expected that was his lot in life. To be the loner.

But something shifted with Ella... And it continued to shift. Like somehow, she's managed to bring him back to life.

Only...he hadn't known he was dead.

But he didn't know what to do with the feeling because it felt like he was fracturing—*and healing*—all at the same time.

Perhaps he should talk to Clementine about it?

Stone didn't have many souls he could confide in, but his sister had always remained one of them. Even when the rest of the pack turned away, she refused to do so.

It only took him a couple of minutes to slide into a pair of light denim jeans and a button-up shirt. He packed a duffle bag full of more clothes, just in case. Since he'd be staying at Ella's house, he figured it was better to be safe than sorry. Especially seeing how uncomfortable she was around nakedness.

When he returned to her Highlander, he tossed his bag in the back and resumed his spot beside her.

"Ready?" she asked, turning to him.

Stone nodded. "Ready. I can direct you—"

"No need," she said, tapping her phone. "I took the

liberty of conjuring up Google Maps while you were inside."

The drive to her house took roughly fifteen minutes since he lived outside of town. He loved being close to the woods and away from prying eyes. He could come and go whenever he pleased and no one would be any the wiser. Especially since he frequently came home without a stitch on.

By the time they pulled into her driveway, Stone's heart was hammering in his chest. She hadn't said a word since they left his house and it was beginning to set off alarm bells.

He reached for her hand as she put the vehicle in park. "Ella, I hope I haven't upset you."

She turned to him, her right eyebrow arching. "Why would you think that?"

"You haven't said much. I thought..." his voice trailed off. He didn't know what he thought anymore.

"I'm not upset, Stone. Not at you, at any rate. I'm just worried. If Silas is cunning enough to oust you, I—" She shakes her head and inhales sharply. "I'm worried about what else he has up his sleeves. I mean, he *killed* the last Alpha. It's kind of a mindfuck. You know?"

Clementine exited the front door, her gaze locked on their vehicle.

"Come on, we better let your sister know what happened," Ella whispered, opening her car door and pulling her hand from beneath his.

Stone swallowed hard, then exited the vehicle. He opened the back and grabbed his duffle bag, tossing it over his shoulder as he followed after her.

"Well? What happened? I'm getting some confusing thoughts from the pack," Clementine said, shifting her gaze from Ella to him.

"Let's head inside," Stone said, tipping his chin toward the door.

Clementine's eyes were wide, but she nodded, then spun on her heel.

"How were the kids? They didn't give you too hard of a time, did they?" Ella asked, glancing around the space.

"They were great. You have two incredibly smart kids." She laughed softly.

A half-smile crept up on Ella's face. "What did they convince you to do?"

Clementine's face took on an innocent expression and even Stone knew whatever came out of her mouth would be full of shit. "Nothing. We just had a great talk."

"Hmmm," Ella said.

"Mom!" Avery shouted from the top of the stairs. "I thought I heard you."

Without another word, she rushed down the steps, taking them two and three at a time. When she reached the bottom, she spread her arms wide, wrapping them around her mother's waist.

Clementine chuckled.

Even Stone found himself smiling at the gesture.

"Where's Asher?" Ella asked, still holding onto her daughter.

"He said something about setting up his computer," Clementine said. "He's come down twice for snacks and drinks."

Ella laughed, and it sounded like music. "That sounds about right," she said.

"So, what happened?" Avery asked, glancing up at her mother.

"Let's sit down," Ella said, pointing to the living room.

Without waiting for a response, she walked to the couch, dropped into it, and sighed.

Everyone else followed after her, including Asher, who emerged from the kitchen with a can of soda in his hand.

"Mom, you're back," he said, cracking open the can and taking a sip. "Does that mean you kicked the other guy's ass?"

Ella lowered her eyebrows and growled, "*Asher*."

He cowered, then grinned sheepishly. "Sorry."

She shook her head, then returned her gaze to Clementine. "Things didn't go as planned. For some reason, I couldn't change. I'm worried that..." Her voice trailed off and she stared at her clasped hands.

Clementine took a seat beside her, then placed her hand on Ella's knee. "It's a big responsibility you've stumbled in on, Ella. You need to stop being so hard on yourself."

Tears brimmed in Ella's eyes and everything clenched in Stone's chest. He wanted desperately to take that pain away.

"What if I can't do it? What happens then?" Ella asked, flitting her gaze from Clementine to Stone.

Stone leaned against the fireplace and shook his head. "That won't happen. The full moon will make sure of it."

"So, the stories are true about that, then?" she asked.

He rubbed at his eyebrow. "I guess they are, yeah."

"Mom, can I TikTok you changing?" Avery asked, her eyes wide with excitement.

It was the first time she'd shown any kind of interest in Ella's imminent change.

Both Clementine and Stone responded in unison, "No—"

Avery blinked back her surprise, then slunk around the back of the couch to sit behind her mom.

Stone pinched the bridge of his nose. "Sorry, it's just—the human world can't know, Avery."

"Yeah, come on, Avery," Asher snickered. "Could you imagine? People would lose their sh—*sugar*."

Ella rolled her eyes.

"It also goes against our Laws. If your mother becomes the pack's Alpha, she'll need to follow these Laws," Clementine offered.

"Stone, you mentioned I could have an advantage with Silas," Ella sighed, turning her desperate gaze toward him. Her features twisted in fear and concern. "Can you explain that now?"

He nodded, then took a deep breath. "Silas attacked Doug the way he did because he knew he didn't have a chance in one-on-one combat. The Alpha —whether Bitten or chosen—has a certain..." His words drifted off as he hunted for the right way to explain.

"The Alpha doesn't need to have strength or size to command respect or obedience. They have an innate power no other member of the pack has access to," Clementine said, helping to finish Stone's thought.

"Where does it come from?" Ella asked.

Stone shrugged. "God, the universe, the moon. Take your pick. No one knows."

Her eyes went distant and she leaned back on the couch. "So, how do I use that to my advantage? We already know Silas isn't going to fight fair."

"I wish I had more answers for you, Ella. But you'll have to lean into your power. You have to hold onto the knowing that this is now your birthright—and no one, not even Silas—can take it from you. That fire will keep you safe," Clementine said, shooting her a reassuring smile.

Ella took a deep breath, running her fingertips along her forehead. "That doesn't really help much."

Stone stepped forward, dropping down in front of

Ella. He planted both hands on her knees and looked up into her frightened face. "You shouldn't worry. You've already tapped into that power."

Her eyebrows scrunched together. "I did?"

He nodded. "Twice. The first time was when you were on the phone with your ex. You tapped into the Alpha command somehow when you told him to shove off." Stone laughed, thinking back to the way it had even made him stop in his tracks. "And you did it tonight, too. Your power was rising when you were about to shift. The power was so strong…" He dropped his gaze, trying to find the words to explain what he felt. "It was like being called home."

Clementine's lips curled into a grin and Stone tried desperately to ignore her.

"When Mom breaks out her *mom voice* everybody runs," Asher laughed. "Mom, you've got this."

Ella looked over her shoulder at her son, and a broad grin graced her face. "Thanks, Ash."

He nodded slightly. "Well, I'm gonna go play some Fortnite. Let me know if you're gonna practice turning into a wolf, though. 'Cause I *gotta* see that."

"Me, too," Avery said, standing back up and placing her hands on her mom's shoulders.

Ella reached up, placing her left hand over Avery's. "Thanks, sweetie. You should go to bed. It's almost eleven."

"Mom," Avery whined, dropping her shoulders.

"At least try," Ella sighed.

"Fine."

Without another word, the two kids left the room, making their way to their bedrooms.

When they were out of earshot, Ella turned to Stone. "If anything happens to me—"

"It won't. Don't even think like that," he said, cutting her off.

"But if it does, I need my kids protected. I'll put some contact details together so you can—"

Stone stood up. "Ella, stop. I refuse to even consider this possibility."

"Give them to me, Ella," Clementine offered, shooting a knowing glance at Stone.

Ella nodded, and relief washed over her.

"I should get to bed, too. Big day tomorrow." Ella huffed out a humorless laugh and stood up. "Can I ask you one more question?"

"Anything," Clem offered.

"What's the deal with Marta? She's not the Alpha or the Beta, but she seemed to be in charge tonight," Ella said, biting the side of her cheek.

Clementine's smile broadened, but it was Stone who answered. "Marta's our oldest pack member."

Ella scoffed. "That doesn't bode well. She's barely thirty."

"She's cute." Clementine laughed. "Isn't she cute?"

Stone nodded, and a smile tugged at his face.

"What's so funny?" Ella asked, confusion written across her features.

"Marta's a lot older than she looks," Clementine said, standing up, too.

The crease in Ella's forehead deepened, but rather than pressing it, she simply nodded. "Well, goodnight, you two. Thank you for being here. Really. I feel much safer knowing you're nearby," Ella said, placing her hand on Stone's shoulder.

The warmth of her palm caused him to shiver under her touch, but he leaned into it regardless.

Clementine's eyebrow arched high, but he ignored her.

"Oh, and there are sleeping bags over there," Ella said, pointing to a stack of rolled fabric.

"Night, Ella. Get some rest. We'll help you practice shifting tomorrow," Clementine said, smiling.

Ella nodded, then retreated up the stairs. For the briefest of moments, Stone wished he was following after her.

He tracked her movements for a few seconds, then returned his gaze to his sister. She crossed her arms over her chest and waited.

Finally, he said, "What?"

"I've never seen you so smitten," she said, smirking. A mischievous twinkle glinted in her eye.

His forehead crinkled and he frowned. "I don't know what this is. It's...*confusing.*"

"The beginning always is," she whispered.

He scoffed, walking away from her as he tried to sort out his thoughts.

"I don't know how to keep her safe, Clem," Stone said, lowering his voice to barely a whisper.

A sad sort of smile crept upon his sister's face. "I understand that better than you realize."

Instantly, Stone felt like an ass. Of course, Clementine understood. She lost the love of her life to the same madman that was after Ella.

He reached out, wrapping his arms around her neck. "I'm sorry. I should have—"

She patted his arm. "Stone, I love you. You know that, right?"

His eyebrows tugged in and he nodded. He took a step back, letting his hands fall to his side.

"Well, then take some sisterly advice, would you?" she said, her expression a mixture of pain and hope. "There's something between you and Ella. You owe it to you both to find out what it is. For all you know, she could be your—"

He shook his head, dropping his gaze to the floor. "Don't even say it."

She laughed and shook her head. "Just because you never found your mate doesn't mean you weren't fated for one. If it's her—"

He glanced up into her green eyes, his heart hammering in his chest.

"If it's her," she continued, "it would explain some things. Don't you think?"

CHAPTER 23

DARK NIGHT OF THE SOUL

ELLA

D o werewolves live longer than humans?

The idea had never occurred to me until a few minutes ago. But if Marta is older than she looks...what else could that mean?

Are werewolves immortal?

My chest constricts uncomfortably and I no longer know which end is up and which is down anymore.

What have I gotten myself into?

To add to the confusion, I have this strange sensation constantly tugging at me to be near Stone. It's like an invisible string is somehow tethered between us, and if I stray too far, it snaps me right back to him. I've never felt anything like that and truth be told, it's not the most comfortable thing in the world.

Be ready.

That can't be a good sign.

Regardless, the sensation has only intensified the more I'm around him.

If I make it through tomorrow night, I'll have to do some digging to figure out what's going on.

I reach the top landing and approach Asher's bedroom. Typically, I'd stop by and say goodnight, but something stops me. Instead, I hold out my hand, reaching for his doorknob. When he's awake, the door is typically open, but it's closed. I take a beat, checking my watch. It's past eleven and I did ask them both to get to bed. Maybe they listened for once. Or at least, want to give me the impression they did.

Yeah, that seems more their style.

Rather than test the theory, I drop my hand and softly pad my way to my bedroom. I doubt I'll be getting much sleep tonight, but I have to at least try. The last thing I want to do is go into a beast battle feeling like the walking dead.

She'll never know...

The words cause me to pause just outside my bedroom door, and I walk back to the railing that over-looks the entry, perking my ears.

What are they talking about?

A shot of panic mixes with my current anxiety and I dig my fingertips into the rail, listening. However, only silence greets me. Then, the light in the living room clicks off.

Shaking my head, I turn back to my bedroom door and walk in.

I catch a strange scent—it's a sweet smell that's far too pungent. By the time the realization hits me —*it's blood*—the door closes behind me and a firm hand grips my throat and pushes me from the entrance.

Flashbacks to earlier consume my mind as I stumble backward. My arms flail around as I try to grab hold of anything that might give me some leverage.

"Finally, we can end this," Silas says, his words dripping with disdain. "I never should have left such an important task to amateurs."

He doesn't have a stitch of clothes on—evidently having shifted recently—and his naked proximity is far too close for my liking.

"How?" I squeak out, fighting back the stars that are trying to claim my vision. I dig my fingertips into his forearm, working on a way to get out of his grip.

Marta was supposed to be watching him—keeping him from doing something just like this. How is he here?

"That old woman doesn't have the power to stop me," Silas snickers, continuing to drag me further into the room.

I must have broadcast my thoughts again. Goddamn it. I need to learn to control that better.

My back slams against the footboard of the bed and I drop my hands, clutching at it for some sort of support.

"No one can stop me. Not her, not you," he continues. "No one."

And yet, you're too scared to fight me fair? I push the thought at him, hoping like hell it pisses him off.

He drops his hand from my throat momentarily, but only long enough to rear up and land his fist across my left cheekbone. Pain flares from the point of impact and I drop against a stack of boxes beside the foot of the bed. Despite myself, I scramble to my feet and manage to put some distance between me and the madman.

"Stone—" I yell. "Clementine!"

A slow grin creeps across Silas's face as he prowls forward. "They're not coming to save you, *woman*."

The word is meant to be an insult, but all I can think about is everyone else's safety.

"What have you done to them?" I spit, fighting back the terror threatening to take me down. If he's done something to *them*... What about my kids?

Oh my god, I *should* have checked on them—

"You can't even shift and you expect to lead the pack. You're pitiful," Silas spits, sidestepping my question.

"Fuck you." I jut my chin out, assessing the boxes from the corner of my eye. I might not be able to shift, but there has to be something in here I can use against him. I need to get to my kids and make sure they're safe.

Silas shudders slightly, then his lips twitch into a

horrifying smile. It's one full of malevolence and lacks any kind of empathy.

"I think maybe I will," he says, violence glinting in his dark, dangerous eyes. "The only question will be— will you be alive for it?"

An icy chill trickles down my spine and I swear my heart stops beating. There's no question he means every word.

"Get off on fear, huh?" I say, anger and terror welling up inside me. "You're sick. You have no right to be the leader of anything."

I clench my fists and close my eyes.

Come on, Ella, fucking SHIFT.

The hairs on the back of my neck rise and a strange sensation floods the room, like an electrical current running alongside water. The sensation is powerful and heady, but when I open my eyes, Silas is even closer and nothing has changed.

A maniacal laugh escapes his lips. "See? Pitiful." He lunges for me, and even his human movements are fluid and incredibly fast.

I push a stack of boxes at him, but he swats at them, barely slowing down. I hop over my antique blanket chest, barely sidestepping Silas's outstretched hand. But somehow, I manage to put myself behind another stack of boxes.

My options are limited. I could dance around him and try to make a run for the door, or I could dive for the window. Neither of which feels like great options, if I'm to be honest.

Silas bounds forward, hopping over the chest and blocking the window.

Door it is.

I knock the stack of boxes over and bolt for the bedroom door. I manage to swing it open before Silas slams into my back, pushing me forward with such force that I lose my balance and land face-first on the landing floor.

Rolling over quickly, I launch my right leg upward and manage to land it right in the middle of his torso as he lunges at me. The impact does little to stop his attack, though. He barely flinches as he flies up and over me, his bits jangling in the air above my head. When he lands on the other side, he doesn't even take a beat to rest.

Downstairs, snarls erupt and something crashes to the floor.

Please, please let Stone and Clementine be okay.

I spin, crawling backward toward my bedroom. Silas doesn't even seem to notice the commotion downstairs. His face is a picture of hatred as his features pinch tight and he crawls forward. His arms outstretch, trying to get a grasp on me.

Apparently, he doesn't even feel it's necessary to change into his wolf in order to beat me.

He's probably right. He's got more mass on me this way.

When I make it to the bedroom, I stand quickly and reach for the door to slam it shut, but he's too fast. Silas is on his feet, too, and he plants his hand on the door, keeping it from closing. Then he yanks it toward him and pushes hard in my direction. The jolt makes my arm give out and the door slams into my forehead.

I blink hard, trying to clear my vision, but the effect is enough for me to lose any semblance of an advantage. Blood trickles over my eyebrow, clouding my left eye.

Silas barges in, and in an instant, his hand entwines with my hair. He continues forward, yanking me damned near off my feet as he drags me right along with him.

I scream and my arms fly to my scalp. "Let me go. Get off."

He slams me into the bed, then pins my bent legs to the edge of the mattress with his knees. He drops down, his body hovering just inches above mine. I try to bring my arms down to fight him off, but he reaches out, capturing them with his hands and locking them in place above my head.

Fuck.

My heart hammers so loudly in my ears, I can barely think. I turn my face away from him, trying desperately to come up with a way out of this.

He's so close I can feel his breath on my cheek as he whispers, "I'm gonna break you. You'll beg for your life—and when you've run out of screams, I'll keep on going just to see how long you can last."

His free hand drops to my neck, his fingertips digging into my flesh. He bends in, licking at the blood on my face and letting out a moan of pleasure.

Tipping his hips downward, he presses his growing bulge against my hip. I fight the urge to pass out, shuddering from the adrenaline and fear.

I've been through a helluva lot, but this—

His fingers drop from my neck to my chest. He palms my breast like he has any right and my stomach rolls. However, I refuse to give him the satisfaction of making a sound.

Grinning to himself, his hand dips downward, and he unbuttons my jeans.

I close my eyes and my brain checks out.

If this is going to happen, I don't want to be here. I don't want any part of it.

I refuse to give him what he wants.

"Mom—" Avery's scream pierces through my brain and my eyes pop open.

There's a scuffle in the landing and I twist in Silas's grip, trying to see what's happening.

"Let her go, you asshole," Asher spits.

I can tell by his tone he's scared, but he's not willing to show it. He's stronger than I am.

He would have been a better choice.

Silas tries to shove down my jeans and my heart just about beats out of my chest.

Fuck no.

We didn't go through hell with Troy only for things to end up like this. The kids deserve better.

I deserve better.

A strange, urgent sense of power builds inside the center of my torso and I lurch forward, about to be sick. The sensation is so intense it's like I'm being torn apart.

Suddenly, the room spins—almost as if it's been sucked down the drain. Every cell inside my body feels like it's pulled apart, spun like a top, then put back together again.

Still fighting the urge to hurl, the motion of it is both incredibly fast and excruciatingly slow.

Then, before I know what's happened, the spinning stops.

When it does, my senses are somehow heightened and I can hear everything—from Silas's jagged breaths to the beating of his black heart. I can practically hear his surprise like it's a physical thing.

"What—no," he mutters, groping desperately at me as he tries to get a new hold.

I can hear the scuffle in the hall with my kids. I can pinpoint every heartbeat and inhale the distinct scent of every being in my home. It catalogs in my brain like it's a magic power I've always had access to.

But more than that, I feel everything, too.

I *feel* one wolf has been taken down in the living room. I *feel* Stone moving through the house and sense his trajectory to intercept my children. I *feel* his plan take down their two captors. I *feel* Clementine subduing another wolf downstairs.

I also *feel* the pack heading our direction like a flare was shot off, guiding them to my home.

Power rolls through us all, like a wave that ebbs and flows.

Then, a vehement snarl erupts from the back of my throat.

CHAPTER 24
BIG GIRL PANTIES
ELLA

Without hesitation, I rear up, kicking with my back legs. The force rocks Silas backward and he stares at me with a dumbfounded expression before he slams into the wall. If he has any thoughts in his head, they fled the moment I shifted.

Good.

I flip over and leap off the bed at him, not wasting precious time. The power and connection running through me, from the pack and back again is enough to guide my actions, even if my logical mind checked out completely.

There's no way I'm not going to be present for this. Silas chose the wrong bitch to mess with and he's going to learn that lesson in true diva fashion.

Before he can shift, I slam into him, all snarls and

raw instinct. My front paws—*so weird*—land just beneath his clavicle and he goes down. Hard.

Unfortunately, by the time I land beside him, Silas's wolf takes his place. He rolls away from me, putting some distance between the two of us. It isn't much, mind you, but enough that we square off.

Standing firm on all four legs, I drop slightly, the hairs on my back rising. Another growl forms in the back of my throat as I take in his every action, assessing his next move.

You can't win. Silas's thoughts jab at me, but they lack any kind of potency. It's like a gnat that floats in front of your face. Annoying, but not that big of a deal.

Funny, I was going to say the same thing to you.

I prowl forward, debating my next move. I could take him down now, or I could wait for the pack. Either way, the results would be the same.

Silas's days tormenting the pack are done. I've decided and just ask my kids—when that happens, there's no changing my mind.

Stone's wolf enters the landing, taking down the wolf hassling Avery. It's not even a fair fight because the man submits almost instantly to him. He didn't even want to be here.

The one tasked with keeping Asher in line, though...

A tussle ensues and Avery screams—though not from her own danger. It's more out of surprise than anything else.

I believe you overestimated your abilities. I say, pushing my thoughts at Silas. I'm sure he can hear the same things I can, which means he knows his numbers are dwindling.

He lurches forward, snapping his jaws and snarling at me.

God, wolves are ugly when they do that. The thought makes me laugh internally since I'm one of them now and must look just as ridiculous.

However, if Silas thought his display would unsettle me, he was sorrily mistaken. I pounce, clamping my jaws on the side of his neck. I rear up, shaking him hard, then I twist, slamming him back down on the ground with a loud thud.

He jerks around, attempting to do the same from the ground, but I manage to stay out of his way. His jaws claim only air.

Out in the hall, a wolf yelps in pain—Silas's guy—and that sweet stench of blood hits my nostrils.

Anger pools in Silas's eyes and he shakes out of my grip. He manages to stand back up and puts a foot or so between us. Then, he darts forward quickly, managing to latch onto the fur beside my shoulder.

A shot of pain explodes across my shoulder, but it diminishes as quickly as it came. He drops his hold, spiraling around and clamping his teeth down on my rear leg. Again, pain erupts, and I drop down onto my backside, trying to drive his head to the ground.

He digs in deeper, drawing blood.

I nearly yelp out from it, but instead, a blast of power rolls out of me like a shockwave. Silas drops his grip, scrambling back and cowering with his tail between his legs.

Whatever I did, it was enough to scare him shitless. I don't even know how I'm doing it, but it's damn helpful.

I limp to a stand, refusing to let his bite be a weakness to me. Or to him.

His fear doesn't last long, though. He races forward, slamming into me. Rearing up, it's a clash of snarls, snapping, and gangly legs as we both attempt to get the upper hand on the other.

Silas manages to catch me by the scruff of my neck. He slams me down hard and my chest tightens from the impact. The hardwood floor in this house certainly doesn't make for a soft landing.

However, I don't stay down long. I'm on my feet again before I've even made a conscious thought to do so.

Anticipation builds in my core.

The pack is nearly here.

Downstairs, Clementine is still fighting with Silas's guy, but she's toying with him more than anything else. From this vantage point, I understand now, the Alpha's mate is a powerhouse all their own. Clementine still has that power innately built into her.

Stone must have known this because she was a damn fine choice to protect my kids. A new level of trust and admiration for him blossoms inside my being.

Snarls erupt in the landing again and Avery screams. I hear as she manages to break from the chaos upstairs, running down to the lower level. Asher follows after her, opting to apparently stick together.

For a brief moment, I wish like hell they were part of this crazy new world so I could hear their thoughts and command them to stay out of the way. However, they both bypass the fight in the living room and lock themselves in the main level bathroom.

Good. That's good.

My attention snaps back to Silas.

Women aren't meant to lead. You know it—I know it. Just submit now and I'll spare the kids. Silas goads, trying to make light of his situation. But he chose the wrong bargaining tactic. Those kids will never be safe if he has his way.

I practically laugh. *You really are a piece of shit. You know that?*

The front door bursts open and more wolves arrive on the scene. They transform from humans to wolves the moment they enter the house almost as if the moon forced them into it.

Relief floods through me when I sense Marta in the lead. Whatever Silas did to get out from under her watch, at least she's still alive.

Others I know by feeling, but not yet by name, arrive. The two women who stood up for me alongside

Marta. A few of the men who backed Stone's play. More yet filed in, and despite not knowing them on a first-name basis, I feel their support. Their trust in me as their leader. Their hope is that this ends the way they think it should.

The thought is trippy but incredibly promising.

They have faith in me and barely know me.

Maybe Stone is right—I should have more faith in myself.

Instead of keeping this fight to myself, I bolt from the room, running past Stone and his current fight. The wolf Stone already managed to submit is cowering in the corner of the landing looking lost and scared with his head down and tail between his legs. For the briefest of moments, Stone's fight halts and the two of them stare in my direction.

As expected, Silas follows after me.

I hit the lower level and back up slowly.

Too scared to fight alone, huh? What a joke. Silas says, prowling down the remaining steps.

If I could smirk, I'd certainly have the biggest one on my face. This dickhead has zero understanding of the way families work. This pack is nothing more than an extension of family and it's clear that when you know that, they'll respect and support you. They're losing respect for him fast.

I guess when you fuck them over—by not following the rules and attacking your own—they're less inclined to see past your differences.

Did you see her eyes?

Forget her eyes...

White?

Deep feelings of surprise, reverence, and even excitement roll through the pack.

I'm not sure if it's a typical response to this type of fight, or if it's because I finally managed to make the shift. Either way, I plan to live up to my role here.

There's no way out of it, so I may as well embrace my destiny. My big girl panties are snapped up and locked in place.

The wolves already in my home spread out, creating a circumference around us at the bottom of the stairs. Those coming in late hover on my porch, constructing a wall of muscle and fur to prevent either of us from escaping.

The only way out is by a winner being declared.

Challenge fucking accepted.

We circle each other in the opening caused by the onlookers. All additional fights have ceased around us and every soul in the area is practically holding their breath. I know, because I can feel it.

My heart hammers in my chest, but every fiber of my being is ready for this fight to be over with.

Silas snaps forward, trying to put me on guard. It's all for show, and even I know that.

At least now he has to fight fair. There are witnesses, after all.

I circle to the left, choosing to go against the grain. Silas follows my lead, rotating counter-clockwise. Each of us monitors the other, watching for signs of weakness or the best place to hit. Silas is predictable, though. He'll go for my injured leg first, which is why I'll give it to him.

Stone's fight upstairs has also halted and he tosses the remaining wolf halfway down the stairs. He stands at the top, and I don't even have to look up to know his intense green gaze is locked on the scene between me and Silas.

Just give in. Submit and we can end this charade now. Silas says, continuing to circle.

I answer by lunging for him.

Biting down hard on his front right leg, I tear back, opening a gash, and flinging blood across the floor. He yelps, but arches around, going straight for my damaged leg, as I knew he would. Before he can make contact, I slam down my backside, smashing his head to the hardwood floor.

Twisting back around, I clamp my jaws onto his throat and squeeze, but he manages to kick me off of him before I can do any real damage. I roll across the floor, scrambling to get back on my feet before he attacks.

Go for his face. Stone's thoughts invade my mind. *Take out his eyes.*

Racing forward, I rear up, battling Silas from my hind legs. Pain burns from my left-hand side, but I stay upright, doing everything I can to get ahold of his face or take out his jugular.

Silas's teeth gnash at me, trying desperately to do the same.

Suddenly, a new surge of power overcomes me and I plant my paw across Silas's face. My claws slash downward, marring his left eye with a huge gash. But the momentum knocks him sideways and he drops like a boulder to the ground.

Blood gushes from Silas's eye, and his head flails around as he tries to wipe at it.

Racing forward, I grab hold of him, tossing him into the railing at the bottom of the stairs. His body hits hard, knocking loose the newel post and a few of the vertical posts beside it.

I let out a soul-splitting howl, announcing to everyone I've accepted Doug's gift. I may not have asked for it, but *it's mine.*

To hell with Silas. To hell with anyone else who thinks they can take this from me now.

I'm the new Alpha in town and I'll protect my own from Silas's fucked up brand of dominance.

Silas tries to rise, but I walk forward slowly, slamming my paw against his neck, and pressing his head down to the floor. It's the equivalent of making him bow before me. At least, that's how I see it.

Stay down. I command.

The powerful wave that rides my words makes every wolf in the vicinity snap to attention. I feel their surprise and their inability to do anything but what I asked.

Silas struggles to ignore the command, but ultimately, he doesn't have the power to pull from. If anything, any power he did have is dwindling fast.

Time to deliver the final blow.

I might be new to this, but you—you're not one of us anymore. You're out, Silas. Take your cronies and leave. The command rolls through me. It's not simply a thought—it's a potent, tangible thing. A commandment he won't be able to ignore if he tried.

The pack shifts, a sense of pride and respect permeating the room. They're backing my play.

Where am I meant to go? I have nowhere. His thoughts are panicked, nearly scrambling, as he tries to find a foothold of some sort.

I couldn't give two shits. It's not my problem. I say, a growl rumbling in the center of my chest.

This isn't fair. I was meant to be—

Another surge of power rolls through me, pulsing outward like a physical force. I'm done messing around. I'm done dealing with him and his whining as if somehow he deserves anything in this life simply because he's him. His reign of terror, of pulling the shots, is over.

Enough. I don't care where you go, but let me give you some advice. It better be as far away from here as you can manage. Pick a new continent. Because if I catch a whiff of you, so help me...no one will be able to find your pieces.

CHAPTER 25
THE NEW ALPHA
STONE

oly shit.

Stone had all but forgotten about the fight he'd been in the middle of. The guy was about to cry uncle anyway, but he had been looking forward to making him do it. The dude actually thought he was only here to keep the kids under control.

What a motley crew Silas had put together.

Stone hadn't cared what the guy wanted. He was here for one thing—to protect Ella and her kids from this very thing.

He was pissed at himself that he missed the signs. Pissed that his Omega status, combined with his rapt attention to Clementine's consideration had distracted him from his job in the first place.

He shouldn't be worried about himself right now.

He should be protecting the new Alpha the way he should have protected Doug.

If there was one thing Stone couldn't live with, it would be failing a second time.

However, the moment Ella shifted, he knew everything had changed. There was an intense charge that nearly knocked them all back. Even Stone had been forced to the ground in reverence and he wasn't even a full-fledged part of the pack.

He'd never felt anything like it.

He didn't have to be a full pack member to know the entire pack felt what he did—and likely more so. It was like a goddess had struck down and announced her presence with a bolt of lightning. It made his entire body hum and even pumped more power into him. Like he was somehow already connected to the Alpha in ways he didn't understand.

Because of that, Stone knew Silas felt it as well, even if he refused to admit it. Or accept it. Silas had no chance to become the Alpha now.

It was predetermined—*destined*.

But that didn't mean he'd stand by and leave it up to fate.

Hell no, he'd hammer the final nail in Silas's coffin if he could.

When Ella's wolf rushed by—everything about her stopped his heart. It was like a piece of his soul had been brought back to him.

He stood there in awe, watching as she ran by.

Her fur was the same white as his and he had no idea what that meant. Up until now, he'd been the only wolf in the pack in two centuries to have white fur. He'd been told it was a sign. Of what, no one seemed to know. As the pack's elder, Marta was the likeliest, but she had also been unwilling to open up about it.

Stone had never felt the need to press her about it.

But now, with two of them, there were more questions.

In addition to her fur, Ella's eyes were striking. They alone would have made him pause.

As she flashed her gaze toward him briefly, he'd been surprised to see one was the color of the sky— bright cerulean blue. The other was a dark, earthy brown. No one else in the pack had two different colored eyes.

However, the biggest head-turner was her size. Despite barely being five foot five as a human, Ella had a good six inches over any of them.

She was fucking massive.

It was kind of glorious to behold. She was far bigger than Doug, even. Far bigger than *any* Alpha he'd come into contact with.

She very likely had no idea just how special she was. How special her *wolf* was.

Granted, he didn't know what any of it meant, but he knew there was significance there. One he'd have to lean on Marta and the other elders to decipher.

It was at that moment, Stone knew she'd win. That question fled the building the moment she shifted and called the pack to her without a single shred of knowledge on how to do so.

It was innate.

Instinct.

A rush of pride coursed through Stone when she had taken Silas down and cast him out. It was fucking karma and despite thinking he'd be the bringer of that hammer, it had come down all the same.

Stone had no idea that day in the woods—when his best friend and brother-in-law was dying—that this strange, awkward woman would hold so much potential.

He had no idea how much he'd come to revere her. To want to be around her.

The instant Ella cast Silas out, the order was pushed to each of them so there was no question. Anyone siding with Silas was out. Anyone questioning her claim could also go.

And now here they were, standing in the middle of the aftermath, waiting for the old to flee and the new to rush in.

Marta stepped forward. *I will accompany Silas to the borders. It was my fault he slipped through. I will not fail you again.*

Seth and a few others stepped forward, parroting their desire to do the same.

Ella prowled the circle, her head high, and her

dominance no longer in question. She tipped her head at Marta and the others, and they corralled Silas and his supporters. The wolves in the doorway opened up, making a path for them to leave through.

Despite being put firmly in his place, Silas still held his head high as he walked out. He should have been respectful, reflective. He should have felt remorse.

Yet, Stone could tell Silas felt none of those things.

Something twisted in Stone's stomach and before he thought it through, he was trotting down the stairs after them.

Ella was kind-hearted, but she didn't know Silas the way he did. If he was left alive, he'd be back. Maybe not now, maybe not even a year from now, but he wouldn't let this thing go.

He'd be back and he'd make everyone in the pack pay.

If Stone followed after, he knew he could put an end to things. Being the Omega of the pack would make it easy for him to carry out the darker deeds no one else would be up to.

Stone? Ella's thoughts pulled him up short. He turned back to face her. *You're not going, are you?*

He could sense the disappointment in her question and it made him pause.

I was going to ensure Silas exits the border. It's all he could think to comment. If she knew what his real plans were, he didn't know how she'd take it.

Marta can handle it. Please stay. It wasn't a command, it was simply a request.

The aftermath of what had just happened was beginning to crash down on her and he could see in her multicolored eyes that she needed someone to lean on.

It was him she'd chosen. How could he not give that to her?

He glanced toward Silas and the other wolves as they vanished into the darkness beyond her street.

Of course. He turned back, making his way to her side.

As much as he would like to go after them—his pull to Ella was stronger. He felt like...even if he wanted to, he wouldn't be able to say no to her. And it had nothing to do with her being the Alpha.

His gaze flitted to his sister.

Could Clementine be right? Could Ella be his fated mate?

The relief that washed over Ella was a palpable thing.

He knew instantly he'd made the right decision.

Two white wolves...

What does it mean?

Maybe so, but...

The thoughts from the remaining pack members began to rumble through his mind.

He knew Ella would be hearing the same thing and she'd have questions later.

Ella began to pace in front of the remaining wolves. He couldn't hear her thoughts, but he could see her conflicted mind was working hard.

Finally, she began to broadcast.

Things are changing. If you don't want to be a part of what I plan on building, you are free to leave. If you want to see what kind of cluster I can whip up, then, by all means, stay. But I promise you one thing... She stopped pacing and sat down on her haunches. *I will not lead the way Silas had tried. It's not how I roll. I'll do things differently. I just hope you'll be willing to give me your patience while I figure out what that means.*

Despite not quite being able to pick up on all of the thoughts, a consensus filtered around the room. That much he knew.

Stone doubted anyone liked the way Silas was pushing things. They were all too scared to say it.

The pack was mostly good people—but they didn't know how to stand up. It's why Stone was cast out instead of Silas. They didn't think evil could worm its way into their midst.

They were obviously wrong.

Now, before you all leave to do... whatever it is you do in the middle of the night... God, I hope it's sleep. She shook her head. *I have one more thing that needs to be done. I have a feeling you all must witness it.*

The remaining wolves began to eye the space, shuffling from one foot to the other in anticipation of what she was about to say. But anxiety unfurled in the pit of Stone's stomach. He had an idea of what might be coming, but he hoped like hell he was wrong.

He needed to take care of Silas before...

An electric charge flooded the room. It was the tell-tale sign that a command from the Alpha was coming. How she'd known how to tap into it without being taught was incredible.

However, he knew he'd never get the chance to go after Silas. Not if he wanted to stay in her good graces. Something big was coming for him and he knew it because he'd felt the same sensations unfolding now, only...in reverse.

Ella stepped forward, staring him in the eyes. *Stone Lachlan, you're no longer the Omega. You're welcomed, whole-heartedly, back into the Black Crater pack.*

CHAPTER 26

DELIRIOUS

ELLA

had no idea if I was doing it right. Truth be told, it all felt a little silly. But I knew it had significance. More than that, I knew it needed to be *said*.

Stone has shown his worthiness over and over again. Anyone with eyeballs can see how much he cares for this pack. Hell, how much he cares in general.

I, for one, couldn't be more grateful to know he's on my side and has my back.

The rest of the pack should be so lucky.

A massive shift takes place, altering the flow of energy in the room. Like, whatever I had said turned a breaker on or something.

Stone's wolf sits down, staring at me. I walk around him, circling him to inspect him for any changes. But I know it's not a visual thing. It's magical.

I live in a fucking magical world.

The concept blows my mind.

"Mom?" Avery calls out, peeking down the hallway from the kitchen. Her wide gaze floats over the sea of wolves in our home and she clutches onto her brother's arm. Sliding behind his back, she doesn't let go of him.

Without thinking about it, I shift back into my normal human form. "I'm here, sweetie." I hold out my arms.

"Mom, get some clothes on. God," Asher says, holding out his hands to block his view of me.

Heat bursts across my cheeks, but I step toward them, ignoring it.

Suddenly, Clementine is human as well. Then Stone...

"Go on home, everyone. We're done here," Clem says, shooing wolves out the front door. She doesn't have a shred of clothes on, but she holds zero excuses for it.

Stone walks to me, ignoring everyone else. His eyes are full of unspoken words that he doesn't bother to release. He doesn't have to.

Asher reaches around, covering up Avery's eyes for her. I drop my gaze and laugh under my breath. This lifestyle is going to take some getting used to.

Most maintain their wolf form but listen to

Clementine as they file out. There's an air of excitement that connects each of them, yet as they go, that energy stays with me, raising my spirits.

When all is said and done, only Clementine and Stone remain behind.

"I'm gonna go get..." Clem begins, pointing to the living room.

Thankfully, since they were here overnight, they both had bags with them.

I nod, shooting them a thumbs up. "Yeah, I'm gonna get dressed, too. Be right back, guys."

My eyes lock with Asher and his lips press tight. He nods in acknowledgment and I make my way past the chaos on the stairs and close the door to my bedroom. The room is a disaster, but at least I'm alive to see it.

Without much fanfare, I rummage for some clothes. It doesn't matter what I wear at this point. It's not like the whole world didn't see all the goods. The mystery has officially flown the coop. Or something like that.

I tug on a pair of sleep pants and a tank top and head back downstairs, completely wired. The remnants of energy from the shift and from everything that happened early still courses through my veins and I have a feeling getting sleep any time soon isn't going to be on the agenda.

When I reach the bottom of the stairs, I flit my gaze around the disaster, shaking my head.

That can wait until tomorrow.

I gingerly step over chunks of wood, padding my way back to the kitchen.

Asher and Avery are hunkered together, digging in one of the boxes and scrounging for food.

Without a word, I reach my arms out wide. They both drop what they were holding and race around the counter. Avery latches on to me first. But it's Asher's long arms that squeeze us all in tight.

"I'm so sorry, guys," I whisper, kissing the side of Asher's face and the top of Avery's head.

Neither of them says anything. Instead, they just hold onto me and I hold onto them.

I can only imagine how traumatic all of this has been for them. And they didn't even witness their mom shifting into a friggin' wolf.

Laughter bubbles up in my chest and before I know it, I can't hold it back.

"What are you laughing at?" Stone asks, entering the kitchen. He's wearing a set of khaki shorts and a black t-shirt that hugs his shoulders and broad chest.

I wipe at my eyes, removing the tears of joy and relief. "All of that and neither of the kids saw what happened with me."

"Did you do it?" Asher asks, stepping back. "Did you turn into a wolf?"

"You could say that," Stone says, nodding. "She was a badass."

"Can you show us?" Asher asks, his face brightening.

I pat him on the shoulder. "Another time. I'm exhausted."

His face falters, but he nods.

"The two of you should go to bed. We can talk about all of this tomorrow," I say, trying to usher them toward the hall.

"But what about the others? How did the guys get into the house?" Avery asks, her voice still higher than normal. "I don't want to go back up there without you."

I tug her in close and wrap my arms around her.

"I found the window they came in through," Clementine says, entering the fray. She's dressed in a pair of jeans and a light-gray sweatshirt that says *Yum* on it. "Looks like the window in the upstairs bathroom was unlocked."

"Is it—?"

"Taken care of," she says, tipping her head. "I also did a sweep. If the basement's clear, there's no one left besides us."

"I didn't hear anyone down there," Asher says.

Clementine winks. "I'm still gonna go check. Which door is it?"

Avery raises a shaky hand, pointing to the door.

With a tip of her head, Clementine walks over to it and vanishes into the basement.

"There, you see? All taken care of. Now, go to bed. This has been a helluva night and you both need your rest. I'll be up soon," I say, stepping to the side and pointing to the hallway.

"But—" Avery starts.

"Bed," I repeat.

If I had been normal, human me, I would have been just as worried as she was. But my senses are still growing and I have no doubts whatsoever that our home is clear.

The two of them nod, making their way out into the hallway.

"Night, kids," Stone calls after them.

They both say, "Night," in unison.

When they've made their way upstairs, I turn to face Stone.

"Well, that was something," he whispers, opening his arms.

I step into his embrace, letting his warmth surround me. Sinking into the feeling of him, I close my eyes, as everything washes over me.

"It's all clear down there, too," Clementine says when she makes her way back to the kitchen.

I pull back from Stone. "Thank you."

"Sure," she mutters, flitting her gaze from me, to Stone, then back again.

"I don't know what I'd do without the two of you..." I say, biting my lip to keep the emotions from welling up. "I'm so glad..."

"Don't mention it," Clem says, planting her hand on my shoulder and walking to the kitchen door.

"Ella, I'm sorry I didn't—" Stone begins.

I plant my fingertips over his mouth, shutting off his words. "You're not all-knowing, Stone. I'm so glad you were here. Thank you for keeping my kids safe."

"But—" the word eeks out, but I press harder and shoot him a death glare.

"You know, Ella... You might be the Alpha, but you still have a lot of work to do," Clementine says, her eyebrows knitting together.

"What do you mean?" I ask, quirking an eyebrow. I mean, sure, I need to learn the job and figure out what the hell is going on here. I'm not dense. But it's clear she has something in mind.

"Like picking your team. We need a new Beta," Clementine offers, a slight smirk gracing her lips and lighting her face.

"There's a lot she'll need to do, but don't over-whelm her already," Stone says, shaking his head.

I didn't put her up to this. Stone's thoughts come to me with more ease and clarity than before.

I smirk at him.

He runs a hand across his neck. It's kind of funny to watch him squirm.

"You and I both know Ella has to get up to speed quickly. Once the other packs know we have a new Alpha, you know they'll be coming to check her out. Some will want to challenge her," Clementine says, matter-of-factly. "It's not often a female is chosen as Alpha."

"Wonderful." I roll my eyes.

"Let's deal with things one step at a time, Clem," Stone says, catching my eye. There's a mischievous twinkle in their depths and I know he's not just talking about my new role.

I point in his direction. "Yes, I agree."

"Fine," she laughs. "But you'll need to face reality soon. This reprieve won't last forever."

"Reprieve? If this was a reprieve, I don't want to know what a shit day is," I mutter.

She chuckles. "I'm gonna go back home. I trust everything is settled now."

Stone nods.

"Night, guys." Without another word, Clementine walks to the front door and out of the house.

The silence that falls when she leaves is more than just from her. The pack brought an energetic safety net—it's the only way I can describe it. It was like having them here meant there was no question we were safe. The level of intensity was a palpable, physical thing.

Now that each of them has left and spread out across our territory, it's more like a blanket or web. It's just as powerful but covers more area.

"What are you thinking about?" Stone asks, turning to me. He lifts his arm, running the back of his knuckles across my cheek.

I glance up, staring into those deep green eyes of his. "I can still feel them. All of them."

A soft smile rises in his features. "It's a wonderful feeling, isn't it?"

"Can you feel it, too?" I ask, placing a hand in the center of his chest. "Right here?"

He nods.

"I didn't expect that." I raise my eyebrows and snicker. "I didn't expect any of this, come to think of it. I'm getting delirious from lack of sleep."

Stone chuckles softly. "I should go. You need some rest."

"Are you sure? You could...*stay?*" I say, biting on the side of my lip.

I don't know what to think about him—or if I'm even in my right mind at this point. All I know is there's something tugging at me to stay near him. Or keep him near me.

I wasn't looking for him. I wasn't looking for any of this. But something tells me, something deep in my core... I was meant for this life.

Stone's eyebrows tug in and he inhales deeply. "I wish I could, Ella. But I need to get to work. My shift starts in an hour."

I blink back my surprise. "What time is it?"

"Nearly six." His soft laugh is like music, but his words don't make sense in my brain.

"No, it can't be..." I shake my head, looking around for a clock. Of course, I don't have one up yet because I didn't have time to unpack my damn house before the werewolf battle.

"And yet it is," he whispers, bending forward to kiss me on the cheek.

I close my eyes, leaning into his touch. Sparks ignite where his skin touches mine and I wish there was some way to keep him here.

"What is this?" I whisper, dreamily.

"Just another day," he says, pulling back. His pupils are so wide I can barely see a hint of green around their edges.

My heart flutters and I grin like an idiotic school kid.

"Well, I look forward to seeing where it leads," I whisper.

"Me, too, Ella. Me, too."

Without another word, he saunters to the door. When he opens it, he shudders into his wolf form. The magic in the moment, in the sensation that lingers in the air, is intoxicating.

He turns his head, his emerald gaze holding my own for the briefest of moments before he takes off running.

I blow out the breath I was holding and stare at the open door.

I've been through some crazy shit in my life...*but this?*

Yeah, it takes the proverbial cake.

Surprisingly no longer worried about my safety, I walk over to the door and close it. I can feel where each wolf of the pack is—including Stone. I also feel their emotional level, if that's even a thing.

There's a low-level vibe of satisfaction running through the pack. Almost as if they've collectively breathed a sigh of relief. They didn't want Silas to be Alpha, either.

If anything were to go awry, this innate sense would alert me before anything could happen. That, in turn, would alert the pack. I'm sure of it.

Flipping the lock in place, I turn around to make my way upstairs. I step over the bits of wood and ascend slowly, my feet only capable of going so fast.

When I look into Asher's room, my heart nearly jumps out of my chest when I realize he's not there. I race to Avery's door and find her missing as well.

Before I panic, a low-level energy pulls at me, and my feet carry me to my bedroom.

There, lying in my bed, are both of the kids. Asher is even facing his sister, his forehead resting against hers as they sleep.

Smiling to myself, I shut off the light and slide in beside them. I snuggle up to Avery, forcing her in the middle, and place my right hand on Asher's shoulder.

As I close my eyes, the realization hits me.

Stone didn't have to go to work.

He knew the kids needed me after a night like tonight. Maybe he even knew they'd snuck into my bed and he didn't want to get in-between us.

I sigh, pressing into my pillow.

If that man isn't careful...he'll do one worse than all of that.

He'll heal my heart.

To be continued...

DID YOU LIKE *MIDLIFE WOLF BITE?*

If so, sing your praises, my friend. No, you don't have to put on a jester's hat or do a TikTok video (though, that would be cool).

All ya gotta do is leave a review.

Thanks for reading! <3

MIDLIFE WOLF PACK
ACCIDENTAL ALPHA · BOOK 2

Midlife can suck it.

Ascending to Alpha of the Black Crater Pack of freaking werewolves wasn't even remotely on my radar. I was just hoping the move to Oregon with my kids would mean less drama than dealing with the ex. Guess that didn't work out.

Now, as it turns out, making friends in midlife is one giant pain in my backside. And believe me, I have enough aches and pains as it is.

While some of the pack is thrilled there's a woman in charge, like the sexy guy I just can't stop thinking about, there's a vocal group who'd rather eat glass than see me succeed.

To top off my stressors, my seventeen-year-old son thinks he wants to be bitten, and this momma is ready to lose her sh—*mind*.

This new Alpha's laying out some new ground rules, so suck it up, buttercup.

Start Reading Now!

A NOTE FROM THE AUTHOR

Thanks so much for reading **Midlife Wolf Bite**, Book 1 in the *Accidental Alpha* series.
This series continues with *Midlife Wolf Pack - available now!*

Join my Patreon to read my books as they're being written (including this series!), get exclusive merch, and to get more news and book-related nerdery from me.

Thanks for being here!
xo Carissa

CAN'T WAIT FOR MORE ACCIDENTAL ALPHA?

If you're waiting for the next installment of Accidental Alpha, check out Carissa's other series.

The Windhaven Witches

Secret Legacy

Soul Legacy

Haunted Legacy

Cursed Legacy

The Diana Hawthorne Series

The Final Five (prequel)

Oracle

Amends

Immortals

Ruins (coming in 2022!)

The Pendomus Chronicles

Trajectory (prequel)

Pendomus

Polarities

Revolutions

About the Author

Carissa Andrews

Sci-fi/Fantasy is my pen of choice.

 Carissa Andrews is an award-winning and international bestselling indie author from central Minnesota. Her books range from paranormal and urban fantasy to science fiction dystopia. Her plans for right now include the continuation of her acclaimed *Diana Hawthorne Supernatural Mysteries* and a new series called *Accidental Alpha*. As a publishing powerhouse, she keeps sane by chilling with her husband, five kids, and their two insane husky pups, Aztec and Pharaoh.

For a free ebook and to find out what Carissa's up to, head over to her website and sign up for her newsletter:

www.carissaandrews.com

patreon.com/carissaandrews

amazon.com/author/carissaandrews

bookbub.com/authors/carissa-andrews

goodreads.com/Carissa_Andrews